PRAISE FOR
The Monsters of Rookhaven

"A stunning book . . .
a brand new take on the monster story."
Eoin Colfer, international bestselling
author of the Artemis Fowl series

"A magnificent, shadowy, gothic adventure full of heart."
—*Emma Carroll*, author of *When We Were Warriors*

"Unique, thrilling, and moving . . . with its timely—
yet timeless—message of choosing empathy over fear,
The Monsters of Rookhaven is proof that Pádraig Kenny
is one of the best children's writers around."
—*Shane Hegarty*, author of the Darkmouth series

"A totally absorbing tale . . .
magnificently illustrated by Edward Bettison."
—*Guardian*

"A wildly imaginative story . . . a triumph."
—*Irish Examiner*

GIDEON

UNCLE BERTRAM

DOTTY & DAISY

PIGLET

ALSO BY PÁDRAIG KENNY

Tin

Pog

The Monsters of Rookhaven

PÁDRAIG KENNY

ILLUSTRATED BY EDWARD BETTISON

HENRY HOLT AND COMPANY | NEW YORK

Henry Holt and Company, *Publishers since 1866*
Henry Holt® is a registered trademark of Macmillan Publishing Group, LLC
120 Broadway, New York, NY 10271 • mackids.com

Our books may be purchased in bulk for promotional, educational, or business
use. Please contact your local bookseller or the Macmillan Corporate and
Premium Sales Department at (800) 221-7945 ext. 5442 or by email at
MacmillanSpecialMarkets@macmillan.com.

Library of Congress Control Number: 2021906616

First edition, 2021
Book design by Rachel Vale and Mallory Grigg
Printed in the United States by Bang Printing, Brainerd, Minnesota

ISBN 978-1-250-62394-2
10 9 8 7 6 5 4 3 2 1

For Catherine, Paul, Fran, and Jean.

Part 1
Someone New

Mirabelle

Mirabelle was in the garden feeding bones to the flowers when Uncle Enoch came for her.

The flowers swayed above her, sniffing the night air. She could hear the creaking of their tree-trunk–thick stalks and the soft, wet sibilance of their petals smacking together as they fed. Though they were nursery plants, each one of them was already over six feet tall, their heads moving blindly in the starry night. A light breeze was blowing. Mirabelle inhaled the air. It was grass scented and warm. Behind her in the great house, she could sense the others stirring from their daylong slumber.

A shadow moved over the moon. Mirabelle smiled as she heard the light flapping of wings and the sound of feet touching the earth.

"Good evening, Uncle Enoch."

The tall, black-clad figure stepped out of the darkness, his wings melting into the air behind him. His pale face was dominated by a long nose. His jet-black hair was pasted back over his skull in a widow's peak. He had an austere presence, but there was genuine warmth in his eyes.

"Good evening, Mirabelle. How was the day?"

Mirabelle sniffed. "Bright and sunny."

Enoch shook his head. "Not my cup of tea."

He reached into the bucket beside Mirabelle, fished out a bone, and threw it up in an arc. One of the flowers whipped forward and snatched it from the air. Another hissed at it, then turned away and went back to bobbing its head.

"They're very hungry," said Enoch.

"They're always hungry," said Mirabelle.

"Like children. Always hungry. Like your uncle Bertram, but with more table manners, perhaps."

Mirabelle took another bone from the bucket. It still had some meat and gristle attached, and for a moment she turned it over and examined it. Enoch watched her.

"I take it you're not tempted to try it."

Mirabelle shook her head. She was never hungry. Not like the others. They frequently spoke about their hunger and their appetites, but Mirabelle never fully grasped what that actually meant. She had never experienced hunger of any kind. Nor did she sleep, either during the day—as the others tended to do—or at night, like the humans in the outside world.

She held the bone up in the air toward the nearest flower. It craned its head down, and she heard the warning in her guardian's voice.

"Mirabelle."

"It's all right," she said.

The flower's head dipped slowly, and it seemed as if its dozen or so companions inclined their necks toward her to have a look too.

As it came closer to Mirabelle's hand, its head unfurled, and she could see the rows of needle-sharp teeth that lined the mouth just where the stem met its petals. With a deft flick of her wrist, Mirabelle threw the bone. The flower snapped it out of midair but kept its head close to Mirabelle as it chewed its morsel. Mirabelle stroked the smooth, leathery petals, and the flower nuzzled her cheek and started to coo. The other flowers followed suit, and soon they were all cooing gently. She smiled.

"So, why are you here, Uncle?"

Enoch stood with his hands clasped behind his back.

"I may have some news," he said, pursing his lips in an effort to hold back a smile.

Mirabelle frowned. "What kind of news?"

"I had suspicions this week about one of the Spheres. It seems my suspicions were correct. We may be about to witness a very rare event."

"No!" she said, dropping a bone back into the bucket without even noticing.

"Someone is coming?"

Enoch smiled now.

"Someone new?" Mirabelle squealed.

Enoch nodded.

"Someone new."

Mirabelle felt a quick fluttering sensation, then her heart started to pound.

"But there hasn't been anyone new since . . ."

"Since you," said Enoch.

"We need to tell the others."

"You can tell them."

Mirabelle nodded, not quite believing what she was hearing.

"Everyone can convene in the Room of Lights as soon as possible."

Mirabelle was already halfway to the back door when Enoch shouted, "Don't tell Piglet."

"Why not?"

"It may well be that he already knows, but it's best not to overexcite him."

Mirabelle nodded. "What about Odd? Where is he?"

Enoch shrugged. "He's on his way."

Mirabelle ran into the house and through the gloom of the dusty, unused kitchen, dominated by its old wooden table. Cupboards lay open and bare, and a single chipped mixing bowl sat forlorn on a countertop.

There was a subtle movement from the top of a cupboard. Mirabelle looked up to see the one-eyed raven looking down at her. It came and went inside the house as if it owned the place. The bird was old and scraggy, and now it blinked its one good eye at her. Its other eye was a blind, milky gray. Mirabelle nodded at it in greeting, and it seemed to regard her with an air of calculated indifference. She grinned, almost compelled to share her news.

She tried her best not to run in the hallway, but she was giddy with excitement. She stopped outside Aunt Eliza's room and pulled at the cuffs of her black velvet dress as she tried to compose herself. She rapped on the door. When there was no reply, she opened the door quietly.

She looked in at the large four-poster bed, its blanket neatly tucked under the mattress. Then at the dresser, with its large vanity mirror and an ornate chair placed in front of it. The dresser was filled with perfume bottles and jewelry boxes and various containers of powder.

Mirabelle sensed movement. She looked to the far-left corner of the ceiling and saw a patch that was darker than the rest.

Mirabelle whispered, "Aunt Eliza, someone's coming. Someone new."

The patch rippled slightly in response, and Mirabelle heard Eliza's voice in her head, the words gentle as butterfly wings beating on a windowpane.

Allow me to make myself presentable, and I'll be there in a moment.

Mirabelle nodded and closed the door.

She felt a strange pressure fill the air, and she tasted the tiniest hint of iron on her tongue as a familiar magic was being worked. She turned and smiled at Odd, who stood before her, the portal by his side already shrinking to a black dot before finally winking out of existence.

Odd was the same height as her, and like her he looked

no more than twelve years old. But he of course was far, far older. He was wearing a bulky sealskin coat that stretched right down to his ankles, heavy mittens, a cap, and goggles. He pushed the goggles up his forehead and brushed snow from his sleeves.

"Where were you this time, Odd?"

Odd frowned. "Somewhere far north. Plenty of snow and ice."

"I can see that," said Mirabelle, her eyes sparkling.

Odd smiled. "You know, then?"

"Uncle Enoch told me. We've got to go to—"

"The Room of Lights." Odd nodded. He'd taken a mitten off and had a finger in the air, as if testing it. "Not long now."

"Tell the twins."

Odd made a face. "Do I have to?"

Mirabelle was already running down the hall. "I'll find Uncle Bertram."

Odd shouted after her. "Whatever you do—"

"Don't tell Piglet—I know."

She slowed down as she reached the yawning opening to her left that led deep into the bowels of the house. She crept past it, one eye on the incline that stretched into the dark. She fought the urge to whisper "Piglet." She remembered the words Uncle Enoch and the others were so fond of using.

Piglet is dangerous.

She turned into the entrance hall and went out through the main door. Her excitement was building. There was a

constant fluttering in
her stomach. She ran
down the steps and
stopped in front of the
bushes. Something
was snuffling in
the undergrowth,
something huge and
hulking rooting at
the soil.

"Uncle Bertram."

The snuffling stopped suddenly.

"Uncle Enoch wants us all in the
Room of Lights."

She saw red glimmering among the leaves, and she heard
a grunt. Her job done, she turned and went back into the
house.

She followed the hallway around, passing the dining
room on her right, before stopping in front of a pair of
impossibly tall double doors at the end of the corridor.

She pushed the doors open and stepped into the Room
of Lights. The towering walls of the cavernous room were
covered in dozens of old portraits that seemed to stretch
upward into infinity. It hurt Mirabelle's neck to look at
the topmost ones, and even then she couldn't make them
out clearly. The ones she could see were stunning in their

variety and strangeness. There was a painting of a man in sixteenth-century dress, his collar a huge white ruffle. He would have been unremarkable except for the three large eyes that took up most of his face. There was a painting of two Victorian ladies in billowing dresses, both of them with four arms. There was a small boy in a white robe, his black eyes expressionless orbs, and four twisting horns on his head.

But most amazing of all were the dozens of orbs of light of varying brightness and color that hung suspended in the air at different intervals and heights.

Enoch called them the Spheres. They were through-ways for her people to come into this world, passages from what was called the Ether. Uncle Enoch had described the Ether as "the place where we are created, where we sleep before birth. A place we have no memory of, but which haunts our dreams."

Mirabelle didn't quite understand it, but she'd read in a book in the library about a place called Heaven, which humans believed was a place they went to after death, and she supposed maybe it was something like that: a grand mysterious idea, unquestioned. She liked the idea of magic, of miracles that couldn't be explained, even among a family as miraculous as hers.

Enoch was already standing before one of the orbs. Dotty

and Daisy, the twins, were with him, their blond ringlets spilling down over their shoulders. They looked like dolls in their matching blue-and-white pinafores.

"Hello, Mirabelle," said Dotty, smiling, her voice timid and quavering.

"Hello, Mirabelle," Daisy sniffed haughtily.

Mirabelle smiled sweetly.

They were interrupted by the sound of the double doors crashing open as Uncle Bertram huffed and puffed his way into the room. In his changed aspect Uncle Bertram was very tall and fat. He wore yellow pinstriped trousers, a red cravat, a mustard-colored shirt, a purple smoking jacket, and a green waistcoat. His large bearded face twitched with excitement.

"How long?" he panted.

"Not long," said Enoch without taking his eyes off the orb. It was a greenish gold, with mist swirling inside. Within the mist was something gray and spindly. Sometimes it looked to be coalescing, then it would become smoky and vanish altogether, reappearing seconds later.

"Oh my, oh my. Imagine if Aunt Rula were here to see this," said Bertram, cramming his knuckles into his mouth in an effort to stop himself from squealing.

Enoch gave a good-humored sigh. "Yes, imagine."

Aunt Rula had lived in the house long before Mirabelle had arrived. Like Odd, she hadn't been very fond of being stuck in one place. One day, she'd decided to go out and travel the human world—and she never came back. Aunt Eliza once confided in Mirabelle that Bertram had been heartbroken. He'd had a soft spot for Rula, Eliza said, and had pined for her for "a hundred years or so." By the sound of it, he was still pining.

The doors opened again, and in swept Aunt Eliza, fixing her hair and patting her long red dress.

"I hope I haven't missed anything," she said, speaking aloud now that her form was fully constituted and solid. She pulled a long glove onto her right arm, and despite her cool demeanor Mirabelle knew she was excited because her arm was undulating as the spiders that made up her body settled among themselves, trying to find their places and form the shape of fingers.

There was another tang of iron, and a black circle formed in midair beside Mirabelle. The circle swirled and grew larger, and Odd stepped through it. Now he was dressed like a Victorian public schoolboy in the customary black jacket with its white collar, along with trousers that stopped at his knees. He twirled his little finger in the air, and the portal suddenly shrank and blinked out of sight.

Mirabelle sighed and shook her head.

He shrugged. "What?"

"Can't you use the door like normal people?"

Odd winked at her. "I can—I just choose not to."

All attention turned back to the orb. Mirabelle could almost taste the expectation in the room, and she was surprised to find she was on the brink of tears. She was moved, but above all she felt an overwhelming sense of pride. This was her first time welcoming a new member of the Family. She wanted to be dignified and calm for everyone. She wiped her eyes quickly, hoping no one would notice.

"This is like your arrival all those years ago."

"I'm sure you were delighted," said Mirabelle.

Odd considered this for a moment. "I've had worse days, I suppose."

"Hush now," said Enoch, "the moment is here."

The orb started to shimmer. Its light was almost blinding, but everyone kept their eyes on it. The gray shape started to solidify, and Mirabelle heard Eliza's voice in her mind now, awe filled and gently hushed.

. . . the youngest of us all . . .

"The youngest must step forward," said Enoch.

Mirabelle didn't even notice who put the blanket in her arms. She stepped toward the orb and held the blanket out between her hands. A small figure emerged from the light. The light faded, and Mirabelle found herself holding a baby in her arms.

The baby had one eye and was covered in gray scales, and when he mewled, Mirabelle could see his sharp teeth. She loved him immediately.

"Welcome," said Enoch. "Welcome to the Family."

Everyone else applauded, apart from Bertram, who was blubbering about how much Rula would have loved to share the moment. Aunt Eliza rolled her eyes, then patted him on the arm.

"And now the once youngest must show our new arrival his home," said Enoch.

They parted for Mirabelle.

"Gideon," she said. "His name is Gideon."

"A good strong name," said Enoch.

"Lovely . . . just . . . lovely," Bertram sniveled, wiping tears from his eyes.

Mirabelle left the Room of Lights, and the first place she went with Gideon was the deepest part of the house. The gloom of the cavernous corridor that led down to Piglet's room was no impediment to her. She stood before the huge iron door that kept him contained.

The child murmured in his blanket and sucked his thumb as she whispered, "Piglet, this is Gideon. He's part of the Family now."

The child's eye turned in wonder toward the heavy door as a great deep moan emanated from within.

Mirabelle smiled, and she chatted to Piglet for a few more moments, while he purred and rumbled contentedly behind the door.

Mirabelle then carried Gideon up to the top floor of the house. She took him to the large window that overlooked the front garden. It was lit by moonlight, and she could see as far as the Path of Flowers. She looked down at Gideon, his single eye now closed, his chest rising and falling as he slept.

"This is your home now," she whispered. "This is the House of Rookhaven. Outside these walls is the Glamour, which keeps our kind safe from the outside world. No one can come in here without our permission. You came from the Ether, and now you're here with us, and we welcome you."

Mirabelle looked out the window and smiled. She felt whole and strong and proud and protected.

But Mirabelle wasn't to know that the humans were coming.

And humans, as is their wont, have a terrible habit of making a mess of things.

Jem looked at herself furtively in the car's wing mirror. By the light of the moon she could see a nose she considered too flat and too broad with too many freckles. Her hair seemed to her to be more rust-colored than red. She felt awful, small, beaten down. Her brother, Tom, was beside her in the driving seat. He'd been trying to get the car started for the past five minutes. Now he sat back with one hand still on the wheel and ballooned his cheeks in exasperation.

"All right, Jemima?" he said. Jem nodded briskly. He only called her by her full name when he wanted to lighten the mood. Tom tapped the steering wheel and tried to smile encouragingly. "It's just petrol. We need more petrol."

Tom was a year older than her, and tall for his age. He looked quite a bit older than his thirteen years, and he carried himself with the swagger of an adult. Even the way he now beat a solid rhythm on the steering wheel reminded her of their father.

His reddish-brown hair flopped in his eyes, giving him a look that served him well. It was a look that fooled strangers, a beguiling charming look, but it didn't fool Jem. She could see the truth in his eyes. The pain, like hers, that he always carried with him.

Jem rummaged in the satchel at her feet and took out a battered petrol-rationing book. One coupon was left, but it was no use here in the middle of nowhere. She showed it to Tom, and he gave a resigned shrug.

He squinted through the windscreen into the night. "We probably should have got some in the last village—" He suddenly gave a great hacking cough, a cough so violent he had to clench the steering wheel with both hands. Jem leaned over to him, but Tom waved her away. The cough subsided. He wiped his mouth with the back of his hand. Jem saw the light sheen of sweat on his pale face, and his eyes seemed to be burning with a feverish light. She remembered the rattling she'd heard in his chest when they'd slept in the car the night before, and just thinking about it made her wince.

"You've had that cough too lo—"

"Too long, I know, I know, so you keep saying, but I'm fine, Jem," he said, trying his best to hide his irritation.

"What now, then?" asked Jem.

"You get out for a bit and stretch your legs. I'll have a rummage in the boot. There might be some petrol in a can buried under all that rubbish. We only need a little bit. We'll be up and running in no time."

Jem nodded, but she knew one of Tom's lies when she heard it. She stepped out of the car while he went round to the back.

They had stopped on a country road bounded on both sides by forest. The road felt too wide and dark. They were too exposed out here. Jem could feel the familiar nagging sense that someone might pounce on them at any moment. There was no cloud cover, and she had to pull her moth-eaten cardigan around her to ward off the slight chill. They'd been on the move nearly six months now since they'd run away from Uncle George. *Uncle.* That was hardly a title he deserved. An uncle was supposed to look after you, not treat you like a dog and thump you for the smallest infraction, and certainly not hit you with . . .

She stopped herself. She shook her head, trying to blot out the memory, but there it was again. Uncle George looming over Tom with a blackthorn stick in his hand, the one that he used to keep his dogs in line. Tom standing straight and defiant, between George and Jem.

"Stop it, Jem," she whispered to herself. She thought about being on the road, about moving on, getting as much distance between them and their old life as possible.

They'd left their lodgings in Southampton three weeks ago under cover of darkness. Tom had woken her from sleep, and they'd crept out of the house while Mrs. Braithwaite the landlady snored upstairs. They'd run out of money again, and Mrs. Braithwaite's suspicions about Tom being younger than he claimed were hardening. No amount of swinging his arms and talking gruffly was going to fool her for long.

They'd moved from town to town, cadging food where they could, with Tom pickpocketing. Jem always played a little mental trick with herself when it came to Tom's pickpocketing. She pushed it into a corner of her mind where she kept the things she didn't want to think about. Things like her dad not coming back from the war, and her mum dying a year ago.

But she was thinking about them both now, and she could feel a hotness in her eyes as the tears began to sting.

That was when she saw it.

Something glittered to her right, at the edge of her vision. She wiped her eyes and looked into the forest. There was darkness there, but within the darkness she caught sight of a brief shimmer.

Jem forgot all her woes and started to walk toward the source of the light. She squinted and caught it again.

She called Tom. She felt frightened but curious. She had to make a concerted effort to stop her teeth chattering. Tom came toward her, muttering something about having to sleep in the car, but Jem ignored him. She pointed into the forest, her hand trembling slightly.

"There's something in there."

Tom narrowed his eyes. "I don't see—"

"There!" Jem shouted.

They saw a brief flickering brightness, like a net curtain blowing in a breeze.

"Do you think we should—"

Tom was already off into the trees, beckoning Jem onward. Jem followed, grateful for the bit of moonlight that lit the way. She was so busy concentrating on where she was putting her feet that she collided with Tom, who'd stopped suddenly. He was too stunned by what he was looking at to notice.

"What *is* that?" he gasped.

Jem stared, but couldn't get her head round what she was seeing.

They were surrounded by forest, but in the middle of the trees was a tall, oval-shaped opening that hovered a few inches off the ground. When Jem walked to either side of it, she could clearly see the forest behind. Yet looking through the opening, she could see a chalk path bordered by

brambles and stunted trees. The long path led toward a large
five-story house surrounded by a wall. The whole image was
slightly hazy, as if covered in filmy cloth. Jem had only ever
been to the cinema once in her life. She'd marveled at the
black-and-white images on the screen, even if the wartime
story had been a little boring. This thing before her looked
something like that cinema screen, but the images were in
color, not black and white, and it all looked very real. There
was no projector here, no dust motes swirling in smoky light.

There's a hole in the world, she thought.

Something else caught her eye. To the right of this
strange opening was a short gray stone pillar poking up

from the earth. The stone came almost to her shoulder and was surprisingly symmetrical and rounded. Various lines and symbols crisscrossed its surface, and the tip of the rock was slanted, with several concentric circles carved into it.

She turned her attention back to the gap. Its edges shimmered white and glowed, flapping and rippling as if blown by a breeze.

Jem blinked and felt a strange wave of dizziness. The dizziness only got worse when Tom stepped through the opening and onto the path beyond.

"Tom, what are you doing? Please come back. I don't think it's safe," Jem pleaded.

Tom waved a hand dismissively while he looked around. Jem clenched her fists, feeling a mixture of fear and annoyance. As usual, Tom was plunging headlong into something without thinking.

"We should go back to the car," said Jem.

Tom shook his head and beckoned her forward.

Jem felt she had no choice. She steeled herself and followed him, lifting her feet gingerly as she stepped over the lip of the hole. Her heart was racing.

The first thing she noticed was the air on the other side. It felt cleaner. She looked back, through the shimmering oval tear, its edges on this side rippling with rainbow colors. She could see the forest, but when she turned round there was no forest, just what looked like a large country estate. There was another stone on this side that looked exactly the same size and shape as the one in the forest.

Tom rubbed his chin. "All right, all right," he said quietly, his eyes narrowing.

"What *is* that?" Jem asked, gesturing at the hole.

Tom shook his head. His cheek twitched, and he gave a nervous little laugh followed by another bout of coughing.

"What do we do?" asked Jem.

"There's a house up there," he said.

Jem shook her head, sorry she'd asked the question.

"Come on, Jem. If there are people in the house, we can ask them if we can stay the night." He grinned. "And if there aren't . . ."

Jem shook her head even more vigorously. "No, we can't."

"I don't see any lights." He shrugged. "We'll be polite and knock first."

Jem shivered and looked back at the dark forest. She supposed anything was better than sleeping in the car again. Also, she thought, there might be the prospect of food. They hadn't eaten a decent meal in two days. Just thinking about it made her belly grumble.

She followed Tom up the chalk path. Brambles were tightly packed on either side of them, and at least a dozen strange leafless trees were arranged neatly along the path's borders, almost as if they were standing sentry.

Tom chatted brightly about how someday they would live in a place just like the house that lay ahead. A mansion, in fact.

She knew his animated talk was just an act for her benefit, something to distract her from the eeriness of what they'd just discovered, so she only half listened as she stared around her.

Tom stopped suddenly.

"Did you hear that?"

Jem held her breath. For a moment there was nothing.

Then she heard it.

A soft rustling followed by a hiss.

The hissing became louder, and Jem caught movement to her right.

All the trees had drooping crowns like snowdrops. Yet they had very few branches. If anything, they looked like oversized flowers.

And now one of them was straightening up. Slowly.

"What's it . . . ," Tom began.

Jem was frozen to the spot. She watched in horrified fascination as what looked like several leathery petals slowly peeled away from each other to reveal row upon row of razor-sharp teeth.

Tom grabbed her arm.

"Run!" he shouted.

Jem turned to run, but Tom was pulling her too hard, and she lost her balance. She fell to the ground. Tom tried to lift her, but one minute he was upright, then he too was on the ground as another plant moved onto the path and wrapped a root round his leg. Jem just managed to reach out and grab his hand before it could drag him away.

She heard a squealing
sound and looked up to see the first
plant moving toward her, its mouth wide open,
a saliva-like substance dripping from its maw, roots
wriggling frantically as it made its way over the path.
"They're everywhere!" Tom shouted.

Jem looked around to see that the rest of the plants
had moved from the fringes of the path too and were
now surrounding them. Their roots were thumping
against the ground, and they were shrieking and
snapping at one another as each tried to be the
first to reach the children.

Tom was kicking furiously at the root
tightening round his leg.

"No!" Jem screamed as she tried to pull her brother away from the creature that had him in its grip.

She looked up. A plant loomed over her, then dipped its head, jaws wide. Jem lashed out at it with her free hand and landed a satisfying smack. It reeled back, squealing, shaking its head, and Jem experienced a moment of both elation and utter revulsion.

A root wrapped itself round her leg now. She held tight to Tom's hand. She punched with her free hand, flailed and screamed, but the more she fought back the more she felt Tom's fingers slip from hers.

She exchanged a look with him. He somehow managed to shake his head. *This is it*, he seemed to be saying.

And then something roared and blotted out the moon.

Jem looked up to see a huge bear towering above her. It roared again. She had never seen a bear in real life before, but she couldn't imagine any bear in existence being as large as this one. It crashed down on its forepaws and bellowed at the plants before taking a swipe at them. The creatures recoiled and shrieked angrily. The bear roared again. They started to retreat to the edges of the path, and Jem saw the root uncoil from Tom's leg, then felt the one holding her release her almost gently. Tom's captor gave a last defiant hiss before it retreated.

The plants took up their sentry positions again. Heads bowed, petals closed, they looked as if they'd never even moved in the first place.

Jem and Tom got back to their feet. Jem felt her throat tighten as the bear turned and bellowed at them, panting furiously, its eyes ruby red, its teeth like yellowed tusks. Jem felt the hot stinking blast of its breath, and as it padded forward, she squeezed her eyes shut and prayed that it would all soon be over.

Then a voice shouted, "Uncle! No!"

Jem opened her eyes. A girl was standing in front of the bear. She was about Jem's age and impossibly pale, with curly black hair. She wore a short black velvet dress with a gray collar. She tilted her head at them, frowning, looking both curious and angry.

"Who are you?"

"I'm Jem, and this is Tom, my brother." Jem was surprised that she managed to blurt out any words at all.

The girl took a few steps toward them.

"My name is Mirabelle, and you shouldn't be here."

Mirabelle

The girl was extremely quiet, and the boy talked too much.

That was the conclusion Mirabelle drew as they made their way to the house. Despite all that had happened to them, the boy seemed a little too confident and chatty for her liking. Even as he talked, she could see him looking around, as if trying to take everything in. It made her suspicious.

The girl, on the other hand, seemed a lot more reserved. She constantly rubbed the cuff of her moth-eaten cardigan between her thumb and forefinger, her eyes flitting nervously between Mirabelle and Uncle Bertram in his bear form. She was still trembling a little, and her clothes were plainly old hand-me-downs. Mirabelle wondered where her parents were. Both of the children looked famished. The boy in particular looked a little sickly and seemed to be relying solely on nervous energy to keep him going.

"We're very grateful to you and your pet bear for rescuing us from those things," said the boy.

Pet bear? Those things?

"Those *things*, as you call them, are the Flowers of Divine Lapsidy," said Mirabelle.

"Flowers? Interesting. I've never come across flowers like that before. What are they exactly? And what is this place? It all seems very—"

"How did you get in?" asked Mirabelle.

"There's a hole in the world," said the girl before her brother could say anything.

Mirabelle locked eyes with her. "A hole?"

The girl nodded, looking almost apologetic.

"Yes, a great big rip in the air. We saw your house through it."

Mirabelle felt a flicker of unease. "Where did you see this opening?"

"At the top of the path where those . . . those flowers were," said Jem.

"Our car ran out of petrol near the spot in the forest where we found it," said Tom.

"So, nobody else from the village opened the way for you?" said Mirabelle.

"What village?" asked Tom.

Bertram gave a little panicked snort, and Mirabelle could feel her own disquiet about the whole situation growing. These two clearly knew nothing about the village of Rookhaven, and the fact that they had somehow passed through the Glamour without the use of a key was not normal.

Uncle Bertram slipped round the side of the house while Mirabelle led Jem and Tom up the steps to the front door. A small flurry of ravens wheeled around the roof, their cawing strange and hollow in the night air. Mirabelle caught sight of their one-eyed leader glowering down from a cornice, then he seemed to lose interest and flew up to join his brethren flitting through the holes in the roof at the far corner of the house.

"This is a very nice place," said Tom, coughing into his hand. "Who lives here?"

"My family and I," said Mirabelle, opening the front door and ignoring his gaze.

They stepped into the cool dark of the hallway. Mirabelle noted the way the two children looked at their surroundings: Jem blinking in disbelief, her mouth widening in astonishment as she took in the vastness of the house before her, Tom looking almost hungry. He wiped a hand across his sweaty brow and seemed to drink everything in. His eyes roved over the staircase's ornate alabaster settings and the convolutions of the chandelier above, its barbed iron arms twisting in and around each other like the branches of a tree.

"That looks heavy," he said.

Mirabelle knew full well that he meant "expensive."

A shadow unpeeled from the murk, and the two children took a step backward as Uncle Enoch revealed himself.

"And who, may I ask, do we have here, Mirabelle?" he said, his voice sonorous but with a hint of steel.

Tom cleared his throat and tapped his chest. "I'm Tom Griffin, and this is my little sister, Jem." He fought back another cough.

Enoch ignored him and instead glared at Mirabelle. "They're not from the village."

"No, Uncle," said Mirabelle. She noted the brief flicker of concern on his face, which only added to the disquiet she'd been feeling since encountering the two children.

She was about to tell him more, but she was taken by surprise when Tom took a step toward Enoch and held out his hand.

"Tom, no," gasped Jem.

Tom ignored her and looked cheekily at Enoch. "And who might you be?"

Enoch raised his head back and looked down his nose at Tom while continuing to speak to Mirabelle.

"How did they get in?"

"They came through the Glamour. I found them on the Path of Flowers."

Enoch looked horrified. "Impossible!"

"That's where I found them," said Mirabelle.

Mirabelle had never seen Enoch like this before. He looked angry and confused, perhaps even a little bit frightened. The sight made Mirabelle feel suddenly cold.

"Strangers," he said, shaking his head in disbelief.

"Perhaps they could stay, just for a little while," said Mirabelle. "Their car has run out of petrol . . ."

Mirabelle trailed off because Enoch looked astounded by her comment.

"They are not from the village," he repeated slowly, as though she had failed to understand something.

"I know, Uncle." She understood his fear, and she shared it, but seeing how terrified the girl in particular had been after the flowers' attack had softened her attitude toward the interlopers.

"Only those from the village receive dispensation."

"I know, but—"

Uncle Bertram burst through the door in his human aspect. He was red cheeked and panting, and he flapped his cravat at everyone.

"Helloooo, I was just wondering what was happening," he said, smiling nervously, twitching all the while. He looked at Jem and Tom. "Ooh, do we have visitors? Where did they come from?"

An exasperated Mirabelle rubbed her palm across her forehead at Bertram's terrible acting.

"We found them on the Path of Flowers," she sighed.

"We?" Bertram squealed.

"I meant me and . . ."

"And your pet bear," said Tom.

"Pet bear?" squealed Bertram, this time looking rather offended.

Tom was coughing again. It sounded as if wet stones were rattling around in his chest. Mirabelle saw the concerned look on Jem's face.

Tom waved his hand at Enoch and Bertram. "Look, we don't want to cause too much"—he coughed again—"too much trouble." Tom almost doubled over as the coughing fit took hold.

Mirabelle wasn't totally surprised when Tom's eyes rolled up in his head and he hit the floor. What did surprise her was how gracefully and slowly he did it, like a ballerina at the end of a performance.

Jem ran to him, shouting his name. She tried to raise him up, but his head lolled back at an alarming angle. She turned to the others, tears rolling down her cheeks. "Help him, please."

No one moved. Both Bertram and Enoch looked shocked.

"Please!" Jem shouted with a sudden fierceness.

Mirabelle went to Jem and helped her hold Tom's head. His skin felt clammy and feverish, and his eyes were rolling behind his eyelids. She saw the terror on Jem's face as she held her brother, the way she looked at him, as if fearing he might vanish at any moment. That's what made the decision for her. She nodded at Bertram.

"Uncle, take him upstairs, please."

Bertram looked at Enoch.

Enoch looked at Mirabelle. "But he's a stranger! He shouldn't be . . . ," he spluttered.

Mirabelle shook her head and turned back to Bertram. She could see the confusion on his face as he seemed to wrestle with some inner turmoil, the slight glimmer of pity in his eyes even while he looked on fearfully. "Please, Uncle. He's very ill. We can't leave him like this."

Bertram looked at Enoch again. "It can't hurt, can it? I mean . . ." He gestured at Tom. "Look at the poor boy."

Enoch looked at Tom. Mirabelle saw her uncle's jaw clench tight and a strange look pass across his face. She couldn't read it, but she could see he, too, was struggling with something, as if he were in pain. Caught between her anger and Bertram's gentle pleading, he suddenly seemed uncharacteristically indecisive. He was about to speak, but as he hesitated, Mirabelle took advantage of the moment to nod at Bertram, who scurried over and lifted Tom into his arms.

Mirabelle directed him toward the stairs and told him which bedroom to use. She nodded at Jem to follow and was just about to step after them herself when Enoch laid a hand on her arm.

"But they're strangers, Mirabelle. From outside."

There was that look again. Mirabelle sensed that Enoch's earlier conviction seemed to be faltering. He almost seemed to be beseeching her.

Mirabelle shook her head. "They need our help, Uncle."

And she followed them upstairs.

Jem

The blind panic that took hold of Jem as soon as Tom fainted was the worst she'd ever felt. It was even worse than the white-hot, nerve-shredding agony of hearing her parents had died. She couldn't lose him too. He was all she had left. She started to tremble uncontrollably and didn't think she'd be able to make it up the stairs behind the man called Bertram who was carrying her brother.

Then she felt a hand on her arm, and she looked into the calm gray eyes of the girl, Mirabelle. Mirabelle smiled.

"He'll be all right."

The trembling started to recede, and Jem clenched her fists to ward off its possible return.

Tom was carried into a bedroom containing a large four-poster bed, a couch, a table, and some chairs that looked as if they had seen better days. Heavy velvet drapes were drawn across the windows, which reached almost from the ceiling to the floor.

Bertram placed Tom gently on the bed, then stood back, looking nervously at Enoch as he entered the room.

Jem found Enoch an intimidating presence, with his dark clothes and cold demeanor. From the way Bertram treated him, it was clear that Enoch was in charge, but he didn't react to Bertram now. He just stood rooted to the spot, staring at

Tom, and even in her anxious state, it was clear to Jem that he was perturbed in some way.

"We need to call Dr. Ellenby," said Mirabelle.

A warm sense of relief washed over Jem when she heard the word "doctor." This at least was something she understood. Enoch gestured for Bertram to come closer to him, and he spoke in hissing whispers. Bertram nodded and left the room. Enoch's eyes alighted on Jem, and she tried to hold his gaze without flinching, knowing that was what Tom would expect of her.

Another gentle pressure on her elbow, and she found Mirabelle guiding her toward a chair that she'd put by the side of the bed. Jem nodded in gratitude and pulled the chair closer to Tom, then reached out and took his clammy hand.

She waited with her eyes fixed on Tom and the rise and fall of his chest. She wasn't sure how much time passed, but she could sense Mirabelle nearby, while Enoch waited by the door. At one point two girls dressed in checked blue-and-white pinafores came into the room. They looked like twins, but Jem paid them little heed, preferring to keep her eyes on Tom. She heard them address each other as Dotty and Daisy, and she could feel their eyes on her as they whispered to each other. Then, almost as suddenly as they'd appeared, they were gone.

Half an hour later Jem heard what sounded like a car stopping outside the house. Bertram came into the room with an older man. The man was elegantly dressed in a brown jacket over a cream-colored waistcoat with dark vertical stripes. He had a neat beard and round glasses. His voice was soothing and warm.

"And what do we have here?" he asked.

"A stranger," Enoch replied, and Jem could feel herself bristling at his use of the word. It seemed dismissive and cold.

"Thank you, Enoch," said the man, heading toward the bed. "Your wildly hospitable attitude to guests is most impressive."

The man held out his hand, and Jem shook it.

"Dr. Marcus Ellenby at your service." He smiled. "And you are?"

"Jem. Jem Griffin."

"From?"

"London."

"Well, hello, Jem Griffin from London. I'm very pleased to meet you."

Jem liked him immediately. He was different from the others. He seemed . . . She struggled to find the word and was surprised by how obvious it was when it finally came to her. *Ordinary*, that was it. He seemed ordinary compared with the people who lived in this house.

He peered at Tom.

"And who might this young fellow be?"

"This is Tom, my brother," said Jem, swallowing hard in an effort to stay composed. The feelings she'd kept bottled up were now bubbling to the surface.

Dr. Ellenby nodded and patted her on the shoulder. He lifted his battered leather doctor's bag onto the side of the bed and set to work. He unbuttoned Tom's shirt and rolled him gently on his side to listen with his stethoscope. Jem's eyes watered as she noticed him pause ever so slightly when he saw the livid scars on Tom's back. To the doctor's credit, he passed over them without comment, and Jem felt absurdly grateful.

He checked Tom's temperature, blood pressure, and heartbeat. Jem noticed the knotted nature of the doctor's long fingers, the large knuckles that looked like bulging points of tree roots, and yet there was a practiced delicacy to his movements.

He smiled at Jem again while he listened.

"A good, strong heart," he said. He put his things away. "It seems young Tom here has a touch of fever. He needs a little rest and some medicine." He took a bottle from his bag and laid it on the bedside table. "This is to be taken four times a day for the next week. And he must not be moved for at least five days. He needs to regain his strength. Which means he needs to be fed." Dr. Ellenby gently pinched a little skin on Tom's arm. "*Well* fed," he said, turning to look pointedly at Enoch.

"A full week?" said Enoch.

Dr. Ellenby nodded, pursed his lips and fixed Enoch with a look over the rims of his glasses.

Enoch sighed.

Dr. Ellenby slapped the side of his bag. "Very good. We'll

see you learn the rudiments of a good bedside manner yet, Enoch." His face crinkled as he smiled.

Enoch shook his head ruefully.

"It's good to see you, Marcus," he said.

Dr. Ellenby nodded. "And you, Enoch. It's been a while."

Jem noticed an odd, strained moment of silence between the two men. Bertram had been quiet all this time, but now he blurted, "It's been quite a few years, hasn't it? We haven't seen you since . . ."

Bertram trailed off as Enoch blinked coldly at him. Jem noticed Dr. Ellenby stiffen slightly, his hand tightening on the handle of his bag.

"Well, then. I'll be off." He nodded at Jem. "Take good care of him now. Keep him fed and rested, and don't take any nonsense from Enoch here. Am I right, Mirabelle?"

Mirabelle grinned at him. "Yes, Dr. Ellenby."

The doctor seemed to hesitate for a moment, then he came toward Jem and squeezed her shoulder reassuringly. "He'll be safe here," he said quietly.

Jem felt her heart sink as she watched Dr. Ellenby leave, though Mirabelle was by her side in seconds, as if sensing her panic.

"You can stay with your brother tonight. Uncle Bertram will fetch some bedclothes for you and will set you up on the couch. Won't you, Uncle?"

Bertram nodded, while Enoch rolled his eyes as he almost glided from the room. Bertram followed him.

"Don't pay any heed to Uncle Enoch. He's just not used to visitors," said Mirabelle. "I'll get you some food from the pantry. What would you like?"

Jem didn't know what to say, but her belly started to rumble. Mirabelle left the room with a promise to be back soon.

She returned a while later carrying a large tray of food. Bertram came with her, carrying a blanket and two pillows, which he deposited on the couch. Mirabelle laid the tray on the table, pulled up a chair, and motioned for Jem to sit.

Jem sat in front of the tray, which was piled with a bewildering mixture of food: sliced beef, apples and oranges, grapes, cheese and crackers, two loaves of bread, several boiled eggs, tea and milk, a bowl of strange brown fruit that Jem had never seen before, a fruit cake, a chocolate cake, and a thing that she recognized as a pineapple, but only because she'd once seen one in a book. She wondered what her mum would have made of all this food. She remembered her bemoaning her meager ration of tea and wondering whether they'd ever see a banana again.

Uncle Bertram hovered nearby, rubbing his hands together in delight, nodding enthusiastically at the food.

"The eggs were only boiled this morning. The beef I am assured is of the finest quality. These are called kiwi fruit. I am told they are of an excellent vintage." He waved a hand airily. "Whatever the term is."

Jem had never seen kiwi fruit before. She'd only heard

of them from their old neighbor Mrs. Tate, whose son had been stationed in New Zealand during the war. Mrs. Tate would read the description from his letters. "Tangy and sweet," he'd called them. The description alone was enough to make Jem salivate. It made her hunger for something more than the gritty coarse bread everyone had to make do with.

But as appealing as kiwi fruit sounded, she decided to go with the familiar. She picked up a boiled egg, keenly aware that Bertram was examining her every move. Her stomach growled as she took the shell off. As she bit into the egg, she thought she heard a tiny whimper from Bertram.

"What's it like?" he asked, licking his lips.

Jem looked at him, feeling awkward with a mouth full of egg. The oddness of the question took her by surprise. She started to munch quickly.

"How would you describe the taste?" he said, wresting a notebook and pencil from his waistcoat pocket.

Jem was at a loss for words. "Eggy?" she said.

"Eggy! Wonderful!" said Bertram, almost bursting with excitement as he scribbled in his notebook.

"Uncle! Please!" Mirabelle protested.

Bertram's mouth and face twitched, and he looked away guiltily.

"Of course, of course. My apologies," he muttered. He moved toward the door. "I would just like to point out that every element of this delicious repast has been sourced by my nephew, Odd. He assures me everything is of the highest quality."

Bertram left the room.

"Like I said, you can stay in this room. There's a bathroom through that door," said Mirabelle, pointing to a door set into the wall on the right.

Jem nodded, unable to speak because her mouth was now crammed with bread.

Mirabelle lowered her voice and looked at her grimly. "You can't leave this room at night under any circumstances, especially after midnight. You must stay in here from the moment it gets dark until morning."

The tone Mirabelle used stopped Jem in midchew. She was aware that her mouth was open, but for some reason she couldn't seem to close it. She only half chewed the wodge of bread and swallowed it. It almost stuck in her throat.

"Why?" she said.

Mirabelle shook her head. "Just please don't leave this room. Promise me, no matter what you hear."

Jem felt a tremor of unease at Mirabelle's tone, but she managed to nod.

Mirabelle looked relieved. "Thank you." She headed for the door. "I'll speak with my uncle and ask him to let you both stay a little longer than Dr. Ellenby suggested."

"Thank you," said Jem. "Thank you so much."

Mirabelle left the room and closed the door behind her. Jem was grateful because she was feeling overwhelmed again, and she covered her face with her hands to fight back tears.

She barely heard the whisper behind her.

"Jem?"

Tom was trying his best to sit up in bed. He looked even more deathly pale than before. Jem ran to him and pushed him gently back by the shoulder. Tom swallowed and looked at the canopy above him in confusion.

"Where . . . ?"

"We're in the house. They're letting us stay. You need to rest."

She gave him some water, which he drank thirstily, then she gave him a beef sandwich, but he only nibbled at it. She saved it for later on a plate by the bed. She gave him some medicine per the instructions on the bottle. It seemed to make him drowsy, and he drifted off to sleep, looking almost serene, less like a boy who'd been burning up from within for days.

Jem organized her own bedding. The couch was huge and looked comfortable. The blanket smelled as if it had been stored in mothballs for decades. Jem fussed over Tom a little, then settled herself on the couch for the night. She pulled the drapes open just a little so that a sliver of moonlight could light her way should Tom need her during the night. She looked up into the dark, her mind fizzing with the sights she'd seen. Whenever she tried to close her eyes, she could see the mass of ravenous flowers, the red eyes of the enormous bear. It took a while, but the exhaustion she'd been battling, coupled with the events she'd experienced that day, finally drove her into a deep, deep sleep.

Jem dreamt.

In her dream, she was too terrified to move beneath the heavy blanket. A shadow had passed over the sliver of moonlight, and somewhere far away she heard a sound like the flapping of leathery wings.

Mirabelle

"No one is eating anybody," growled Mirabelle.

She glared across the dining room table at Daisy, who smirked in response.

"It was a reasonable question," said Daisy, pouting.

"Was it a reasonable question?" asked Bertram a little too hopefully, as he looked at Enoch sitting at the head of the table with Eliza.

"They can leave as soon as the boy wakes," said Enoch.

"Dr. Ellenby said he needs a week to rest," said Mirabelle.

"Can we eat them then?" asked Dotty sweetly.

Mirabelle slammed her palms down on the table. "I told you already!"

Dotty's eyes brimmed with tears, and her lower lip started to quiver. Gideon, who had been gnawing on a bone in a corner behind Mirabelle, looked up and frowned.

"Absolutely not. Mirabelle is right," said Bertram. "It would be rude." He nodded and looked very gruff and serious, then he seemed to reconsider. "Would it be rude?" he asked, looking hopefully again at Enoch.

Mirabelle could feel a tightness in her chest. She glowered at the twins and Bertram.

"We used to hunt humans," said Daisy gleefully.

"This is true," said Eliza.

"And they used to hunt us," said Dotty, looking cowed and miserable.

"Which is why we have the Covenant to maintain balance and peace between us. We do not encroach on them, and they do not encroach on us. We stay within the confines of the Glamour. That is the agreement we made with the humans generations ago, and we must respect it," sighed Enoch.

"The agreement was made between us and the village. They're from beyond the village, and I know the Covenant extends to not hunting anyone in the outside world too, but they came to where we live, not the other way around, so maybe we can eat them," said Daisy.

"That's a technicality, and you know it," Mirabelle snarled.

Daisy shrugged, and it took all of Mirabelle's strength not to leap across the table and shake her.

"I can't even remember what human flesh tastes like," said Eliza.

As if on cue Gideon gave a tiny belch.

Mirabelle turned to Enoch.

"We need to help them," she said.

"And we all need to agree on the best way to deal with this intrusion from the outside world," said Enoch, rocking back in his chair in exasperation. "Where is Odd?" he shouted.

"We don't need Odd," said Mirabelle.

"My dear Mirabelle, as senior member of the Family—"

Mirabelle hopped off her chair. "You're not the most

46

senior—Piglet is the oldest. And they should be welcomed by us. Strangers or not."

Enoch gave a sardonic smile. "As you know, Piglet is little better than a child when it comes to matters of governance."

"Governance!" Mirabelle snorted.

"What's governance?" Dotty whispered to Daisy. Daisy shrugged.

Enoch was struggling now, his face a mass of tics and twitches. "Mirabelle," he growled.

"*No one is eating anybody*," said Mirabelle, her chest so constricted with fury it felt as if she might never breathe again.

"In fairness, Mirabelle, you're not *able* to eat anybody," said Daisy.

This time it was Enoch's turn to slam the table. "*Where is Odd?*"

Bertram pointed toward the ceiling.

All eyes looked up as a black swirl grew just inches beneath the ceiling and the portal opened. A small figure fell through it and landed with a crash on the table.

Odd stood up and dusted himself off. He picked up a bright red fez, which he'd dropped in his fall, and placed it back on his head. He frowned and pointed to his right, then his left.

"I think I need to reassess my entry points," he said.

Enoch glowered at him.

Odd looked at everybody. "What are we all here for?"

"We have guests," said Mirabelle.

"*Uninvited* guests," said Enoch, giving Mirabelle a haughty look.

"Guests we can't eat," said Bertram, jigging up and down in his chair.

"A young boy and girl came through the Glamour," said Eliza.

"That's impossible," said Odd.

"So we thought," sighed Enoch.

"Apparently there's a tear in it," said Eliza.

Dotty and Daisy clutched each other and whimpered. Uncle Bertram started sucking his thumb. Enoch closed his eyes and looked pained.

"A tear?" said Odd. "That's not good. I've never heard of anything like that happening before. Can it be repaired?"

"Yes," said Enoch. "Although it might take some time."

"That means anyone can get in, doesn't it?" Dotty whined.

There was a moment of silence as they all considered this. Eliza shifted uneasily in her chair, and Bertram, without looking at her, reached out and held her hand. Enoch looked troubled. Mirabelle caught his eye, and immediately he straightened up, masking his concern. He cleared his throat.

"We will deal with the problem, and with our visitors," he said.

"I see," said Odd. "So we repair the damage to the Glamour and send our uninvited guests on their merry way?"

"The boy is sick, Odd," said Mirabelle. "They have no one else."

She gave him a pleading look. Odd looked at her sympathetically and nodded. He walked across the table toward Enoch. Enoch looked at him with suspicion, then Odd sighed, took the fez off, and laid it on Enoch's head. Enoch blinked in disbelief. Mirabelle thought she might explode with delight. Gideon had clambered into her lap, and he looked at Enoch, his eye shining with wonder.

"A gift for you, Uncle," said Odd. "An act of generosity. Perhaps you can see your way to a generous gesture of your own."

Enoch looked at Mirabelle as she clamped a hand to her mouth and tried not to laugh. He glared up at Odd, then ripped the fez off.

"Perhaps," he hissed.

Odd bowed then made a circle in the air with his little finger. A portal opened.

"Now, if you'll excuse me, I need to go upstairs."

Odd entered the portal, and it winked out of existence. A second later there was a clattering sound as something hit the floor of the room directly above them. All eyes looked toward the ceiling, and there was a muffled "Ouch."

Eliza tutted and shook her head. "He needs to learn to use the stairs."

Enoch looked at Mirabelle. "A week and no more," he said.

Mirabelle nodded, her lips clamped together tightly to stifle her glee. She squeezed Gideon to her and he hugged her back.

Mirabelle and the others left Enoch and Eliza to discuss the matter of the Glamour. Mirabelle thought Enoch looked particularly troubled, but she presumed he would figure out a way to fix it. There were ways she knew nothing about, magic she had heard whispers of that could be worked to fix it. Of that she was certain. Bertram was worried that the flowers might go wandering into the outside world. Enoch reminded him that, like them, the flowers were bound by the Covenant and their own promise to protect the path.

It was near dinnertime, so Mirabelle made her way to the larder at the back of the house and opened its once-green door, now peeling paint and gray with age.

Mirabelle walked in and was greeted by the smell of raw meat. Four slabs of ribs hung from hooks in the ceiling. Mirabelle wheeled a handcart out from the corner, unhooked the smallest slab, and plonked it onto the cart.

"Mirabelle."

Odd was standing in the doorway, holding a coconut.

"A coconut," he said, smiling as he held it up for her to see.

"I can see that, Odd. Why do you have a coconut?"

Odd deposited it on a shelf. "Uncle Bertram asked me for something 'interesting' to test his palate."

"You've been away a lot recently," said Mirabelle. "Where've you been?"

"Oh, you know." He shrugged. "Here, there, and everywhere."

Mirabelle smiled at him. She couldn't help herself. There was something amusing about the studied seriousness of Odd's face that contrasted so sharply with his boyish appearance. But most of all, Mirabelle was delighted to see him. Of all the inhabitants of the house, Mirabelle's bond with Odd was the strongest, though Piglet was a very close second in her affections.

As if on cue, there was a low, mournful howl in the distance.

"He's hungry," said Odd.

"Isn't he always?" said Mirabelle.

She pulled the cart out of the larder, and it trundled and squeaked along the hallway. Odd fell into step with her.

"Morocco," he said suddenly.

"What's that?" said Mirabelle.

"I was in Morocco, and Tunisia, and a place that might have been Greenland, somewhere by the Russian steppes, and an island," said Odd, counting the places on his fingers.

"Sounds lovely," said Mirabelle.

"Oh, and Gateshead," said Odd.

"Why Gateshead?" Mirabelle whispered.

Odd just shrugged. He reached into his pocket and took out a smooth black arrowhead.

"I found this." He rummaged again. "And this," he said, taking out a lump of something yellowish and gray.

"What is it?" Mirabelle asked.

"Soap," Odd said brightly.

"You go around collecting soap now?" said Mirabelle.

"Only old soap," said Odd.

"I see," said Mirabelle, smiling and shaking her head.

"I don't think I've anything else of interest," he said, doing another rummage. He took his hand out of his pocket, and there was a delicate gold chain on his palm. "How did that get in there?" he muttered. He frowned as he put it back in his pocket.

They walked in silence for a moment, then Odd said, "Do *you* think we should eat the visitors?"

She knew he was only teasing, but Mirabelle gave him a pained look.

"I mean, surely it's a valid question," said Odd.

"Do you want to eat them?"

Odd chuckled. "Not particularly."

"On principle?"

"Oh, but of course," said Odd.

Mirabelle smiled.

Odd seemed to consider something for a moment. "I mean, we have vowed never to eat them, and in truth, having spent some time among them during my many travels, I do rather feel a certain sort of benevolence toward them."

They were quiet again, and then Mirabelle felt a rushing sensation, a sense of rightness.

"We should help them," she said.

Odd pursed his lips and looked thoughtful.

"We should, Odd. They're not from the village, but that doesn't mean we turn people away. Family or not, they deserve our help."

Odd nodded.

They continued along the hallway with only the rumble of wheels and the squeaks of the cart punctuating the silence.

"How is Enoch?" asked Odd after a while.

"Enoch is Enoch." Mirabelle sighed.

"And you've been out and about," he said.

"I have."

"Seen anything interesting?"

"The outside of the house. The inside of the main wall. The garden."

"And you haven't been tempted to go farther afield?"

"I'm not like you, Odd. I don't have a special talent like yours that has to be indulged just because Enoch says it would be 'unnecessarily cruel' to limit it. The rules actually apply to me."

"I see you didn't answer my question," he said.

"I'm not allowed to go *farther afield*."

"Again, not an answer to the actual question I asked."

They arrived at the long, wide corridor. Piglet's deep moans floated up the passageway. They reached the iron door moments later. At twenty by twenty feet, it towered above them and was decorated with monstrous figures. Tentacled, horned, many-winged, several-eyed. All twisted and turning in a maelstrom of claws and teeth. Jagged runes were scratched in between the figures. No one really knew who had created the door. No one knew how old it truly was. But everyone knew its importance. Sometimes Mirabelle just liked to stand and look at it and try to take all the images in, as if attempting to interpret an ancient language.

She pointed at it. "I like to think this is a story of sorts. All these pictures."

Odd tilted his head and looked at the door. "So you've mentioned before. Perhaps it is."

Mirabelle whispered to herself. "But what the story is I can't really say."

She squinted at the images again. She always felt compelled to look at one particular figure, though she hated it. Amid all the teeth and claws was what looked like a bony creature with its flesh sloughing off, right at the center of the chaos. It had a long face and empty eyes, and it seemed to be howling as it held smaller creatures in its claws. Its mouth was jammed with dozens of long sharp teeth, and it looked as if it were bringing the smaller creatures toward its shrieking mouth. It was strange. It was the only image on the door that never failed to make Mirabelle's skin crawl.

She pointed at the creature. "I wonder what that is. It looks horrible."

"Indeed it does," said Odd, looking both repulsed and thoughtful.

Mirabelle laid her hand gently on the cold metal.

"Piglet?" she whispered.

There was a sudden pounding from behind the door as something heavy drummed the earth, getting closer and closer. It was followed by an almighty clang and a deafening roar as the door shuddered.

Mirabelle smiled. "Piglet."

She turned toward the cart, ignoring the howling and snuffling behind the door, and spotted Odd motioning with his hand. A black hole started to open in the air beside him.

"Where are you going?" asked Mirabelle, a little exasperated.

"I don't know," said Odd casually.

"Will you be gone long?"

Odd stepped into the dark portal, turned around, and shrugged. Both he and the portal winked out of existence.

Mirabelle groaned in frustration. Behind her, the door vibrated as Piglet hurled himself against it, claws scraping the other side, howling and bellowing.

Mirabelle tipped the meat out of the cart, toward the panel at the bottom of the door. She turned the keys sticking out at both ends and flipped the panel down. Immediately there came a horrendous snuffling at the gap, and the frantic expulsion of Piglet's hot, short, almost panicked, breaths.

Mirabelle rolled the meat onto the panel, flipped it back into place, and locked it. She sat down and leaned against the door, listening to Piglet's loud whimpers of pleasure, the smacking of lips, teeth tearing meat, splintering ribs.

"How are you, Piglet?"

There was a response, like a dismissive groan, as Piglet concentrated on his meal. The snuffling and gobbling recommenced.

"That's nice to hear," said Mirabelle. She usually gave Piglet a moment as he ate, but today she felt a strange pressure in her chest, and the words were out before she knew she'd said them.

"We have visitors, Piglet. They're human, and they're not from the village, but I think they need our help. The boy has old scars on his back, and the girl looks like . . . She looks small and fragile, as if . . ."

Mirabelle faltered. She felt a strange mixture of sorrow and anger when she thought about Jem and her brother.

"They just need our help, I think. Enoch doesn't like them because they're not from here, but surely you can't turn people away if they come looking for help?"

Piglet's chewing seemed to become quieter, more contemplative. Mirabelle imagined he was listening to her. She would often come here and sit and talk to Piglet for hours on end. She knew he couldn't speak, but there was something comforting in the way he seemed to listen. "Sympathetic," that was the word Eliza liked to use when describing Piglet—although Enoch would sneer at this. Mirabelle sided with Eliza. Piglet didn't judge anyone. Piglet had no ax to grind. Piglet was never mean to anybody.

Piglet is dangerous.

Uncle Enoch's words rang in her ears. She knew that

Enoch meant well and that he was only protecting everybody, but somehow Mirabelle knew Piglet was decent at heart.

There was a rippling, bubbling belch from behind the door, and Mirabelle laughed. Piglet started to pant, and Mirabelle could hear him moving away from the door.

She stood up. She felt the runes and figures that stood out in relief upon the door's surface. There was no sound from Piglet now. It was as if he'd suddenly winked out of existence too. She leaned her forehead against the coolness of the metal and closed her eyes and whispered.

"Piglet?"

She strained to hear, thinking that maybe there'd been a sound, like sand swirling in a sea breeze. Mirabelle smiled.

"Thank you for listening, Piglet. Thanks for always listening. We'll talk again soon."

Was that a low, distant moan she heard? Like a whale humming deep in the ocean at night. Mirabelle took a step back from the door. Once again her eye was drawn to the creature at the center of the frenzy of monsters on the door. Sometimes she was convinced it was moving, but that was obviously a trick of the light.

She turned to wheel the cart back to the larder, resisting a strange urge to look back over her shoulder at the door.

Piglet

Piglet revolves in blackness.

He likes it here. He likes listening to Mirabelle's voice, soft and warm and flowing gently into that dark like a glittering rainbow. Mirabelle is like a light as fierce as the light of stars, and when she goes, he misses her, but he knows she will be back, just as he knows many things without being able to put words to them.

Sometimes Piglet feels like the moon, vast and shining. Other times, he is like a speck of dust in the dark. Lost. Alone. But he is never afraid.

Ever.

Piglet has never known fear. He has known hunger, he has known curiosity, but when it comes to fear, he has only ever known the fear of others. "Piglet is dangerous," they whisper, and Piglet doesn't understand the words, but he smells the fear; he can almost taste it. Fear tastes funny. Not like meat.

Piglet likes meat. He likes it most when it's warm. It's always tastiest when it's alive.

Piglet listens now.

Piglet is always listening.

He hears every voice in the house, and because he hears them, he is never truly alone here in the dark.

Tonight he has heard something different.

The two new hearts Mirabelle told him about are thrumming on the air.

Piglet holds his breath. He listens hard. Piglet likes to know things. He knows more than most, having been here since . . .

Well, since what seems like forever.

The two hearts are not like the ones he is used to. Piglet listens for a while and wonders what this means. Then he remembers he is hungry. So very hungry.

Piglet is always hungry.

He groans and rolls over in the blackness, trying to ignore the rumbling in his belly. He sharpens his teeth and claws. He yearns to be about in the world outside. Out where the meat is, where the blood flows. Warm and sweet and delicious. And because Piglet doesn't belong to the past, the present, or the future, because he is beyond time, he sees things others cannot see, knows things others cannot know. And now he knows one thing above all for certain.

Piglet knows that very soon he will be free.

Part 2
What Piglet Saw

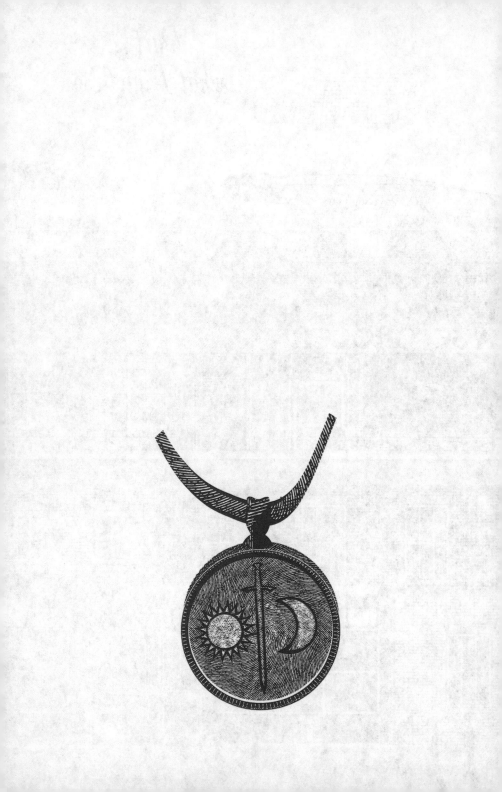

Mirabelle

It was delivery day.

Mirabelle always liked delivery day. It meant she had a good reason to leave the house. It was always a relief to go outside, because she sometimes found the darkness inside the house stifling. The windows stretched from floor to ceiling, but every one of them was covered with heavy drapes, and even the air felt thick and deadened. She'd already taken her stone pendant. It was a small disk looped into a leather band that hung from her neck. She liked to trace the symbols on its surface with her fingers: a sickle moon and a burning sun facing each other, separated by a sword. According to Eliza, these were the signs that afforded the wearer protection from sunlight. Enoch made the stone pendants, the lore passed down through generations of the Family. Although they preferred not to be out during the day, family members used the pendants to move around or migrate in the outside world.

Mirabelle was heading for the front door when she saw the girl.

"Hello," said Jem, looking a little lost and nervous.

"Hello, Jem," said Mirabelle brightly.

Jem gestured around her with a finger. "I was just walking . . . I didn't . . ."

Mirabelle nodded. "That's okay. We can't expect you to be cooped up in your room all day."

The girls looked at each other across the hallway. There was an awkward silence.

"How's your brother? How's Tom?" asked Mirabelle.

"Sleeping."

Mirabelle nodded. "Good."

Mirabelle was pleased to see Jem smile a little at that. It was a shy smile, but a smile all the same.

"It's delivery day. Come and meet Freddie," said Mirabelle.

"Yes, come and meet Freddie," said Daisy, her transparent head suddenly sliding out from the wall to Jem's left.

Jem shrieked and recoiled, almost tripping over her own feet in fright.

Daisy stepped out from the wall, became fully corporeal, and pouted at Jem.

"Aw, diddums, aw we afwaid?"

Mirabelle clenched her fists and hissed, "Stop that, Daisy. She's a guest."

Daisy raised an eyebrow as she looked at Mirabelle.

"Our *guest*? She's no better than an intruder. Intruders shouldn't be welcomed. They should be punished."

Mirabelle saw the fear on Jem's face.

Mirabelle advanced on Daisy. "You leave her alone. If you don't, I'll throw you in with Piglet."

Mirabelle felt a warm twinge of pleasure as she saw Daisy's mouth twitch.

"You wouldn't."

Now it was Mirabelle's turn to raise an eyebrow.

Daisy pointed at Mirabelle for Jem's benefit. "She can't sleep. She can't eat. And this is her only aspect. She can't even turn into something interesting, or do anything useful like walk through walls. She's worse than your kind. She's so boring."

Jem looked completely confused by all this.

Everything Daisy said was true, but that didn't make the sting of the words any less harsh. The rest of the Family each had at least one discernible talent, whether it was turning into a bear like Uncle Bertram, or Odd's ability to travel wherever he wanted in the blink of an eye. The others also had at least two aspects to their appearance. Eliza could take human form, while at rest she was a swarm of spiders. Even the twins could change their appearance. Mirabelle had nothing. She'd looked the same ever since she'd emerged from the Ether.

Mirabelle took a deep breath and was about to say something to Daisy, but was interrupted as a panting Dotty stepped out of the opposite wall.

"Found you!" she shouted, pointing at Daisy.

Mirabelle brushed past Daisy and took Jem by the elbow.

"We're coming with you," Daisy called after her.

"No, you're not," said Mirabelle. "It's daytime—you should be sleeping. Besides, you don't have your pendant."

"But we wanted to see the visitor," she whined. "We couldn't help it. We wanted to see."

"We smelled her," said Dotty, exchanging a sly grin with Daisy.

Mirabelle flashed them both a warning look and turned away with Jem.

"How can they do that? How can they move through walls?" whispered Jem. She still looked a little shaken.

"It's their talent," said Mirabelle.

"A talent?" she said, looking back warily over her shoulder.

"Yes, we all . . . well, most everyone in the house has a talent. I'll explain later. Let me introduce you to Freddie."

She tried to put Daisy's words about her lack of any special gifts out of her mind as she gently urged Jem toward the front door.

The sun was shining outside, and a cream-colored van was parked close to the door. The van had FLETCHER's painted on it, although the brown lettering had faded in some places. It belonged to Mr. Fletcher, the local butcher. Along with Dr. Ellenby, Mr. Fletcher and his son were the main points of contact between Mirabelle's family and the human village.

Uncle Enoch was deep in conversation with Mr. Fletcher himself. Fletcher was a bald, bull-necked, barrel-chested man, shorter than Enoch, but no less intimidating. To Mirabelle he looked like a volcano perpetually on the brink of eruption, rubbing his thumbs against his fingers, twitching as though he suspected someone might be making a casual slight against him. He hadn't always been like this. Mirabelle remembered him before the war. He'd been different then.

Freddie was at the back of the van loading cardboard boxes onto a hand trolley. He was thirteen years old, lean and wiry. He tended to keep his head down and his shoulders hunched, as if always expecting a blow.

"That's Freddie," said Mirabelle to Jem.

"Fweddie Weddie," said Daisy, suddenly sashaying balletically in front of Mirabelle, waggling her own stone pendant in Mirabelle's face.

Mirabelle wrinkled her nose. "Behave, Daisy."

She noticed Mr. Fletcher turn to look at Jem before he and Enoch continued their discussion.

"They're talking about me," said Jem, fiddling with her cuff again.

Mirabelle thought about lying to her to make her feel better, but decided against it.

"Yes, they are," said Mirabelle, "but they're also talking about the Glamour."

Jem looked confused.

"The Glamour is the magical barrier that protects our home from the outside world. Only Dr. Ellenby has the key. He gives it to Mr. Fletcher every delivery day. That way he can enter. You and Tom came in through a tear in the Glamour's fabric located right at the spot where Mr. Fletcher usually unlocks the way in. Uncle Enoch thinks the magic there has become worn, like the handle of an old door that's been open and shut over too many years," said Mirabelle.

"Magic?" said Jem, looking a little stunned.

"Yes," said Mirabelle, realizing the enormity of what this meant for Jem.

"Magic, I never would have imagined . . . It just seems so—"

Dotty came over and whispered into Mirabelle's ear.

The three girls looked at Jem's feet and her tattered brown shoes. Mirabelle felt guilty when she saw the look of embarrassment on Jem's face.

"You're standing on Great-Uncle Cornelius."

It was clear that Jem had no idea what she meant, and for one awful moment Mirabelle worried Jem might think she was making fun of her.

Jem looked down. There was a dark patch on the ground. A blob that looked as if it might have the approximation of a human form if only its lines were a little sharper.

"He wasn't wearing his protection," said Dotty, displaying her pendant.

"So he burned," said Daisy with a little too much relish.

"Up he went like dry kindling," said Dotty.

"I heard him screaming," said Daisy almost wistfully.

"It was a long time ago," said Mirabelle.

Jem stepped off the silhouette with a look of horror on her face.

"This is Freddie," said Mirabelle brightly, waving a hand

in Freddie's direction as he came toward them with his hand trolley piled high with boxes.

"This is Jem, Freddie," said Mirabelle. "She's staying for a while."

Freddie seemed briefly surprised by Jem's presence, then gave a quick nod and mumbled, "Hello."

Jem nodded in return, and the twins giggled. Mirabelle tried to ignore the twinge of annoyance she felt and focused all her energies on Freddie.

"Would you like some help?"

The boy shrugged. "If you like," he said quietly.

He pulled the trolley backward up the steps, and they all followed him into the cool dark of the house.

Dotty and Daisy whirled in and out of the walls, keeping pace with the others. Mirabelle noticed how unsettled Jem was by all of this, and she smiled encouragingly at her, while trying to hide her growing irritation at the twins' interrogation of Freddie.

"How are you, Freddie?"

"Are you well?"

"We missed you last time."

"It's lovely to see you again."

Freddie kept looking straight ahead, the gentle rumble of his trolley echoing and bouncing off the walls.

They all made for the larder. Freddie opened the doors with the practiced weariness of someone used to doing the same task over and over again. Mirabelle shoved herself into the larder beside him and helped unload the boxes. Jem followed suit. Dotty and Daisy stayed outside, giggling to each other.

Mirabelle watched Freddie as they worked. He looked so much like his brother James now that he was older. It was something she'd remarked on once and then immediately regretted when she'd seen the look of absolute devastation on Freddie's face.

She thought about James and his easy manner, how he'd always had time for a chat. He'd been tall and handsome with the brightest blue eyes she'd ever seen, and he and his father used to have such a laugh with each other when they came to drop off deliveries. Freddie would come along too. He was just as quiet and shy in those days, but he'd found it easier to smile and look people in the eye. And from the way he'd looked at James it was clear that Freddie had worshipped his older brother.

Then there came a day when James didn't turn up and there was only Freddie accompanying his father. Mr. Fletcher told her proudly that James had gone off to fight in the war.

Much like the one that had come before, the war never touched them in the house. They got snippets of news from Mr. Fletcher, but nothing more. He was bullishly cheerful about their chances. "We'll show them" was the phrase he used most often. Even Freddie seemed to have a zealous light burning in his eyes, and he carried himself proudly whenever James was mentioned.

Sometimes Mirabelle would stand by one of the high windows at night and look at the white flashes in the distance, over Southampton. She imagined the quiet crump of bombs and the mournful howl of air-raid sirens, and she wondered why people felt compelled to fight each other. It was something she just couldn't understand.

Uncle Enoch said it was the humans' war, and it had nothing to do with them. But that didn't stop Mirabelle feeling sorry for them and wondering what made them hate each other so.

She was thinking about all this when Jem dropped one of the boxes. It hit the floor with a *pop* as one of the corners burst open. Jem tried to lift the box, but this only allowed a slab of raw meat wrapped in greaseproof paper to fall out and hit the floor with a *smack*.

Everybody froze.

Daisy moved first. As quick as a darting serpent, she became transparent and passed right through a horrified Jem. Daisy's eyes bulged as she reached for the greaseproof bundle, but Mirabelle was quicker and snatched the package off the floor.

"No!" she said.

Jem was leaning one hand against a shelf to support herself while she clutched her chest. She was panting hard.

"Did you see what she . . . She went through . . . She . . ."

Mirabelle looked at Freddie, who was frozen in place, fists clenched as he stared at Daisy. Daisy's pupils were expanding, and her eyes were now almost completely black. She pulled her lips back, and Mirabelle could see the teeth sharpening.

"No, Daisy," she hissed.

Daisy's eyes went to the package in her hand, and it was only then that Mirabelle saw the blood trickling out of the paper and down onto the floor. She shook her head at Daisy.

"No."

Dotty was sidling round the larder door, licking her lips and growling. Jem was still panting and wincing, completely oblivious to what was unfolding right in front of her.

"Get out," Mirabelle said to the twins.

Daisy rubbed a hand across her mouth and started to advance toward Mirabelle.

"OUT! NOW!" Mirabelle shouted.

The twins stopped moving. Daisy's face twitched, but she finally relented and stepped out of the larder, ushering Dotty away with her, all the while keeping her eyes on the package in Mirabelle's hand.

Mirabelle shoved the wrapped meat back inside the box, then went over to Jem and took her by the arms.

"Are you all right?"

Jem nodded. She looked extremely pale.

"She's not supposed to do that," said Mirabelle. "Sorry."

Jem swallowed and stood a little more erect, straightening her cardigan. Freddie kept his distance and remained quiet, giving both girls time to compose themselves before they all headed back toward the front door.

They walked some way down the empty hallway before Daisy popped out of the wall again and fell into step beside them. Mirabelle could see the smirk on her face, and she felt the whisper of air behind her that announced Dotty had joined them too. She took a deep breath to suppress her anger, knowing full well that Daisy would be looking for the first chink in her armor to provoke her.

Daisy being Daisy, though, was willing to fight a battle on all available fronts, which was why she targeted Jem next.

"It's a courtesy shown by the people from the village," she said, grinning at Jem.

"What is?" asked Jem.

"The meat. The boxes of meat. I know you're thinking with rationing still going on, why are they having all that meat delivered? We could probably get it by other means with the help of Odd, but the more senior members of the Family prefer to stick with this so called *sacred* agreement cos it's gone back generations. The people of the village of Rookhaven have given us meat for a very, very long time, and because of that, we've agreed to leave them alone."

"Daisy!" Mirabelle growled.

Daisy ignored her. "Like I said, it's a courtesy. Some might say a necessity, in case we might be tempted to look *elsewhere* for food. We can only really enjoy raw meat, you see." Daisy's smirk returned, and now her eyes were hard and bright as she looked at Freddie. "Freddie's just continuing the family tradition by helping his father with his deliveries. Isn't that right, Freddie?"

Freddie kept his head lowered as he pushed his trolley. They'd reached the entrance hall now, and Freddie picked up his pace.

Daisy ran ahead and stood against the front door, blocking his escape.

Mirabelle could feel her head starting to spin as rage wormed its way through every nerve ending.

"Freddie's very good for bringing us deliveries," said Daisy.

Jem looked lost as she glanced from Daisy to Freddie. Freddie stared at the floor, biting his lower lip, his knuckles whitening.

"You're nearly as good as your brother, James," said Daisy.

Freddie flinched as if he'd just been punched. His shoulders sagged, and he looked as if his legs might go out from under him. The fury Mirabelle felt was cold and tingling.

"He was very good too," said Dotty in her whispery, awe-filled voice.

"We miss him. Do you miss him, Freddie?"

"You do miss him, don't you?" said Dotty. "Of course you do. He was very nice, always polite and smiling. Such a pity he had to go away and fight in the war . . ."

"You leave him alone!"

Even Mirabelle was shocked by the source of the voice. She turned to see Jem, ramrod straight, her face white with anger.

Daisy tilted her head. "*What* did you say?"

"I said, 'Leave him alone.'"

Jem was shaking. Her transformation was dramatic enough to make even Mirabelle forget her own fury for a moment.

Daisy moved away from the door and took a step toward Jem. "You can't talk to me like that."

"I just did," said Jem, standing her ground.

Mirabelle smiled at this response. Even Freddie was fascinated now.

No one said anything. Mirabelle felt as if a thundercloud were rolling in from the horizon, announcing a storm.

Daisy narrowed her eyes and licked a corner of her mouth, eyeing Jem like a predatory tiger.

"Do you feel sorry for him because you're just like him in some way? Is that it? I mean you look sad and pathetic, like you've lost something too. Or should I say . . . *someone*."

Jem lowered her eyes and took a step back. Mirabelle felt her heart sink.

Daisy stepped closer to Jem.

"Was it your father? Is that who you lost?" Daisy pouted. "Aw, poor widduh diddums, did you wooze yo daddy in the waw?"

Jem refused to look at her, and she wiped her eye with the cuff of her cardigan.

"So small and mortal and weak. I feel sorry for you, little girl," said Daisy. "And now look at you, sniveling like a—"

The slap Mirabelle delivered to Daisy's face echoed through the hall. Mirabelle didn't know whether she was more surprised or Daisy. Daisy blinked and put a hand to her cheek. Black dots danced in front of Mirabelle's eyes. She wanted to do it again, and she raised her hand, not even sure what she was doing. Daisy became almost completely transparent. She laughed in Mirabelle's face. A horrid, angry laugh. Mirabelle couldn't help herself and swung a fist, but it passed right through her. Daisy circled her and laughed again. She called her names, called Freddie a crybaby, called the humans pathetic. Mirabelle didn't hear most of it. She was still too angry, and the world was flaring around her.

"Can't catch me, can't catch me," Daisy chanted.

Mirabelle dived and just passed through Daisy again.

"Can't catch me, can't catch me."

Mirabelle saw Daisy's pendant dangling from her neck. Uncle Enoch had used a special combination of spells to ensure that the twins' pendants would always stay in place whether they were corporeal or not. Mirabelle grabbed at it. Daisy snarled, swerving out of the way, and resumed chanting, "Can't catch me," as Mirabelle swiped at her again and again.

At last Mirabelle managed to grab the stone pendant

with both hands and started to twist Daisy around by the leather band. This only made Daisy shriek with delight as she continued her chant.

At the rear of the hall was a full-length mirror that Aunt Eliza liked to use when she was prettifying herself for a night walk. Mirabelle kept whirling Daisy around, keeping in mind the exact position of the mirror, moving closer to it with each arc.

She felt her rage swell to bursting now, paired with a delicious joy at the sudden look of terror on Daisy's face. Daisy's mouth formed an O. Mirabelle could see her trying to concentrate, but she was moving too fast, and Mirabelle had already made her decision when Dotty shouted, "Mirabelle! No!"

She swung Daisy round with all her might. Daisy flailed as she tried to stop her momentum, but it was too late for her to materialize now. She hurtled toward the mirror and fell right into it. The pendant hit the surface of the mirror, fell down the length of it, and clattered onto the floorboards.

Mirabelle could see Daisy floating on the other side of the mirror, pounding her fists against it and shouting, but she couldn't make out the words.

And, just as quickly as it had come, Mirabelle's anger was gone.

Daisy howled silently beneath the mirror surface. Suddenly she was jerked left, then right, by some unseen force. She scrabbled at thin air with her hands, like a swimmer fighting a riptide, and then she was whipped away, dragged backward into the depths, until very soon she was little more than a dot in the distance.

There was stunned silence in the hall.

Until Dotty screamed.

Jem

Jem had been rooted to the spot in terror when she saw Daisy get trapped in the mirror. The running in and out of walls was terrifying, as was the thought that someone could be incinerated by sunlight, but this was somehow worse. The screaming from Dotty shook her out of her paralysis, as did the sudden entrance of Enoch bursting through the door with Mr. Fletcher close behind.

"What's going on?" Enoch demanded.

Dotty pointed at Mirabelle. All she could manage was "She . . . she . . ." and then she burst into tears.

Enoch towered over Mirabelle. Jem could see the defiant set of her jaw as she looked up at her uncle, and some small part of her almost cheered.

"What happened?" said Enoch.

Mirabelle pointed at the mirror. "Daisy's in there."

Enoch looked bemused for a moment, then he strode over to the mirror and picked Daisy's pendant off the floor. He looked at the mirror surface and squinted.

"How did she get in there?" asked Enoch.

"Muh . . . Muh . . . Mirabelle threw her in when she wasn't solid," Dotty wailed.

Enoch turned and looked fiercely at Mirabelle, but Mirabelle didn't seem fazed.

"Is this true?" said Enoch.

Mirabelle nodded.

Enoch looked at a loss for a moment as he considered this piece of information. He turned to Mr. Fletcher, who, along with Freddie, seemed to regard the whole episode as nothing out of the ordinary. Jem was amazed by their lack of surprise. For her own part she was almost dizzy with a strange mixture of terror and confusion. Yet these people were talking as if it was an incident involving children bickering over toys.

"I'm sorry, Mr. Fletcher. We may have to continue our discussion at a later date."

Mr. Fletcher simply nodded. He grunted something to Freddie, and Freddie followed him out of the door, casting a quick glance at Jem as he left. Jem noticed the way they both walked, plodding, slightly hunched, as if they each carried the same heavy weight on their shoulders.

A woman dressed in a purple evening gown dashed into the hallway, clutching an ornate silver hand mirror.

"How did Daisy get into my mirror?" she asked.

Enoch sighed and gestured for her to give it to him. He looked at it, and a corner of his mouth curled up. He turned the mirror round so that Mirabelle could see.

Daisy was shrieking silently inside as she pounded on the surface of her prison with her fists.

"She'll be traveling through all the mirrors in the house now." He looked accusingly at Mirabelle. "You know how dangerous it is for her to pass through the surface of a mirror. She could be trapped for who knows how long."

Dotty couldn't take it anymore, and she ran sobbing toward the back of the house.

"How terrible for poor Daisy," said the woman dryly.

"This is serious, Eliza. It's unconscionable behavior."

"Sorry, Uncle," said Mirabelle, bowing her head.

"We'll have to get her out of there," said Enoch, looking into the mirror.

"How, pray tell?" asked Eliza.

"Odd will help," said Enoch.

"He may be busy. We might not want to disturb him," said Eliza.

"That's right. He has a lot to do," said Mirabelle.

Enoch held the mirror at arm's length as if appraising himself. He seemed to consider what they were saying.

"You know, it might not be that urgent," he said, looking a little distracted. Daisy was mouthing the words "Help me." Enoch cleared his throat and tugged at his collar as if remembering his place. "But this is very serious, Mirabelle."

Mirabelle clasped her hands in front of her and nodded. She looked penitent, but Jem had spent enough time with Tom to know when somebody was pretending to be sorry.

"This cannot go unpunished. Odd will be found, and he will correct this." Enoch looked again at the mirror. "Soon," he said, a little too hesitantly.

Jem saw Mirabelle and Eliza share a look of amusement. Enoch turned a withering glance on her.

"This is family business. Perhaps you'd like to retire outside for a little while."

Jem knew an order when she heard one, but found she couldn't leave, not like this, not when Mirabelle needed someone to stand up for her. She felt sympathy for her in dealing with the twins, despite the rather unnerving end result. She felt the overpowering need to say something. She turned to look at Enoch.

"She was only sticking up for me and Freddie."

Enoch seemed momentarily taken aback, as if he was offended that she'd had the temerity to speak to him. Eliza looked impressed with her intervention.

"That's all she was doing," Jem said, holding his gaze for as long as she could. When she finally turned to leave, she saw Mirabelle smile at her in gratitude.

She stepped into the sunlight and was surprised to find Freddie coming up the steps.

"I was coming back in," he said.

Jem nodded, unsure of what to make of his anxious demeanor.

"Just to say . . . to say thank you," he said.

Jem nodded again, feeling a little stupid and at a loss for words.

"For standing up for me," he said. He didn't seem to know where to look, and he gave a nervous nod before heading back down the steps. At the bottom he stopped and looked back up at her.

"Who was it for you? Who did you ..."

He couldn't seem to look directly at her, and Jem felt a sudden tautness in her chest.

Who did you lose?

"My dad," she said. She tried to add *and my mum*, but it seemed too much to say, as if the words might be so heavy that they would drag her right through the earth and she would end up falling and falling forever.

Freddie nodded in understanding. "Sorry," he said.

He headed back to the van, where his father waited, eyes fixed forward, unblinking, unseeing.

Jem sat on a step and watched the van drive away. She felt cold despite the shining sun, and she tried to look straight ahead and not think of anything.

"He took my pendant."

Jem jumped at the sound of the voice behind her. Mirabelle was standing just inside the door.

"I'm sorry," said Jem.

Mirabelle shrugged. "What do you have to be sorry for?"

"I annoyed Daisy in the first place."

Mirabelle sniffed. "She annoys everybody else. She deserves everything she gets."

"Do you want to come outside?"

Mirabelle shook her head. "I can't. I need my pendant to protect me out there."

Jem looked at the dark patch on the ground where Great-Uncle Cornelius had allegedly once stood. She tried to imagine what it meant to go unprotected in sunlight for someone like Mirabelle. She found it difficult to imagine, but that didn't stop her shivering.

"What will happen to Daisy?" she asked.

"She'll float around in the mirror realm until someone is sent to get her out. She and Dotty are usually very careful around mirrors."

"Mirror realm?"

"It's the place behind all mirrors apparently. Nothing much there, or so people say. Odd has been, I think. He says it's very boring."

"I see," said Jem, although she didn't really. This was just another very strange piece of information that she was finding difficult to digest.

"Uncle Enoch says that he doesn't want you wandering around the house on your own," Mirabelle said, then winked at her and waved her inside. "But he didn't say anything about a guided tour."

Jem went inside, and Mirabelle took her hand.

"Come on. Let's show you around, Jem Griffin."

Freddie

If there was one thing Freddie Fletcher was used to, it was silence.

Silence was the great suffocating thing that had squeezed itself in between the cracks of his family since his brother had died, and it had grown, like a great fungal mass filled with poison. Freddie knew that to ask the wrong question was to risk releasing all that poison, so he hardly ever spoke to his father, least of all on delivery day.

But today felt different. They'd collected the key from Dr. Ellenby, who didn't think they'd be needing it, but gave it to them anyway, "in case Enoch has done his work and fixed the problem." They didn't question this curious statement.

Freddie's father had allowed him to hold the key as they drove away from Dr. Ellenby's. It wasn't a conventional key. It was a palm-sized gold disc made of bands of concentric circles. Freddie had seen his father place it on the pillar in the forest dozens of times. Just holding it made him instantly feel more grown up. He'd hoped that today would finally be the day his father asked him to fix it in place and turn it, opening the way to the Path of Flowers. But any illusions he'd had about doing so were dashed when they arrived at the stone.

Now they understood what Dr. Ellenby meant by "the

problem." They'd never seen this strange tear in the Glamour before. Both Freddie and his father were slightly stunned, but they drove up the path anyway, the flowers bobbing their heads as usual, as if in greeting.

Freddie couldn't get the colors around the fringes of the tear out of his head—beautiful shimmering rainbow colors that danced in the air—yet he couldn't shake the feeling that the rip was an omen of sorts.

"I can take the key back to Dr. Ellenby if you like, Dad?"

Freddie was as surprised as his father at his own offer. His father looked at him, then nodded.

"Just be quick about it."

He parked the van outside their butcher shop and handed the gold disc to Freddie.

"Be careful now," he said. "Don't lose it."

"I won't," Freddie replied.

His dad grunted and clambered out of the van, heading toward his shop.

Freddie got out and walked away from the butcher's and up the main street. He enjoyed walking. It allowed him time to think. It made him feel lighter.

The street was bathed in sunlight, and he could see Constable Griggs across the road talking to Mrs. Smith the greengrocer. Both of them waved and he waved back.

Ahead of him Alfie Parkin was standing outside Nicholson's Bakery. Alfie was about a year older than James would have been . . .

Freddie winced inwardly, forcing himself to stop thinking about it.

Alfie leaned heavily on the cane he'd had ever since he'd come back from the war. Freddie had never got used to seeing him with it. He remembered Alfie being at least two stone heavier before the war, fit and active, messing about with James, not this wan, sickly figure.

There was always a moment when Freddie's eyes met Alfie's and Freddie would have to steel himself to say hello, hoping and praying that Alfie didn't see the pity in his eyes.

Now, as Freddie watched, Alfie hovered outside the baker's, seemingly considering whether to go in or not.

Freddie felt that he had to do something. He readied himself, keeping his voice light and friendly.

"All right, Alfie? You going in?"

Alfie turned, looking slightly mortified.

"All right, Freddie. Yeah, just thinking about what I might buy."

There was an awkward pause, and Alfie gave an embarrassed smile. Through the glass of the door, Freddie could see Amy Nicholson behind the counter. She was serving his neighbor Mrs. Arkwright. There was no mistaking her vivid white hair and faded pink coat. She was chatting away. Freddie could see her hands flapping in the air and her rapid nodding. "Mrs. Arkwright could talk for England," his dad always said.

"A sticky bun maybe?" said Freddie.

"Maybe," said Alfie, biting his lower lip as he watched Amy serve the old lady.

"Right." Freddie smiled.

Alfie limped toward the door, and Freddie fought the urge to open it for him. He heard Amy's voice as she greeted him, and the shy hesitancy of Alfie's response.

Freddie walked on.

He was at Dr. Ellenby's front door minutes later. He knocked and was surprised when the doctor answered in rolled-up shirtsleeves, puffing on his pipe.

"The key, Dr. Ellenby."

Dr. Ellenby nodded in gratitude, his eyes twinkling. "Good lad, Freddie. Thank you," he said as he pocketed the disc.

Freddie blushed a little.

The doctor narrowed his eyes and looked at Freddie.

"You all right, young man?"

Freddie swallowed and nodded. Dr. Ellenby had this effect on you. He was kind and disarming, and you always wanted to confess everything to him. Freddie didn't want to say anything, though. He decided the best way forward was to distract him.

"There's something wrong with the Glamour," he said.

Dr. Ellenby frowned. "So you saw it, did you? I thought Enoch might have fixed it by now."

Freddie nodded.

The doctor sighed. "I suppose there'll have to be a council

meeting." He shook his head and muttered to himself. Freddie knew the doctor wasn't too fond of the council, even though he himself was a senior member. It consisted of the few townsfolk people considered best suited to the task of liaising with Mirabelle's family and ensuring the Covenant was observed. "Self-important stuff and nonsense for self-important men," he'd once said in Freddie's presence, and then immediately apologized because Freddie's father was also on the council.

"I should get home," said Freddie.

"Thank you for bringing the key back." Dr. Ellenby closed the door. For a moment Freddie just stood there, feeling a sudden urge to knock again and tell him everything.

About Dad. About Mum. About how sad the world feels now. How sad it's felt since . . .

Freddie shook the thoughts from his mind and headed toward the green. He stood on the corner for a moment and noticed something blue and red in the mud where the grass had become scarce.

He nudged it with the toe of his shoe and realized it was a small Union Jack. No doubt a remnant from V-E Day, when the whole village had gathered on the green to celebrate.

The whole village.

That wasn't strictly true. He and his mum and dad had stayed at home. Freddie had felt separated from the world that day. The sound of celebrations had carried on the wind, ghostly and faint, like something from a dream. Adults singing, children laughing as they ran around the green. Out his bedroom window he saw people make their way home, smiling and laughing. He'd spotted Kevin Bennett walking with his parents. Kevin had only been five years old then. He'd waved up at Freddie, and Freddie had waved back, smiling at Kevin's shiny red cheeks and how breathless he looked.

Then Freddie had spotted Mr. and Mrs. Smith, both looking lost, stooped and tottering along almost aimlessly, their flags by their sides. They were returning to a house that would never see their sons walk through the front door again, and he felt that familiar sensation of something heavy weighing him down.

Later that same evening, Freddie had gone for one of his walks as dusk settled over the village. The streets had been eerily empty, and as he'd walked by the Smiths' house, he'd heard sobbing coming from a front room.

Freddie had heard enough adults weeping behind closed doors to last him a lifetime.

He looked at the village green now and tried to imagine the V-E Day crowds, tried to imagine their joy. He tried most of all to imagine what that joy felt like, but he couldn't.

Freddie took one last look at the empty green, then turned and headed home.

Jem

They were in the main hallway when Mirabelle raised a finger in the air.

"Shh, listen," she said.

There came a delicate tinkling sound of metal on metal. Jem followed Mirabelle's gaze up to the iron chandelier. It was hard to be sure, but she thought she saw something moving.

Whatever it was suddenly leaped from the chandelier and plummeted toward them. Jem shrieked and jumped in response. Mirabelle laughed, and Jem felt her cheeks flush with a combination of embarrassment and fear.

The thing that dropped from above had wrapped itself around Mirabelle's neck. It had a tail. It was nuzzling under her chin, and Mirabelle was chuckling.

"Stop it, Gideon."

Curiosity finally overcame Jem's fear, and she stepped closer for a better look. The wiry, gray-scaled creature was no bigger than an infant. It was wearing dark trousers that stopped just above its ankles, a dark jacket, and a shirt with a stiff collar. Each foot had three clawed toes. There was one eye in the center of its forehead, and the creature chittered amiably as Mirabelle stroked under its chin with her index finger.

"This is Gideon, the youngest member of our family," said Mirabelle.

Jem looked at Gideon, her heart pounding. She thought she might react with horror, but instead the strange wonder she felt surprised her.

"How old is he?" she asked.

"Not that old at all. He arrived quite recently. He came from the Ether. He's small now, but he's growing quickly. He can already walk and climb. He might grow to be as big as me or as large as Uncle Bertram. Or he might stay the way he is now." Mirabelle shook her head. "It's hard to predict what final form you eventually take after you come from the Ether. Odd has looked the same way since he emerged about three hundred years ago."

Jem nodded, as if she knew what Mirabelle was talking about. She saw the amused look on Mirabelle's face. "I'll explain it all later."

She gestured for Jem to follow her, and they walked side by side down the hallway. Gideon burbled contentedly as he rested on Mirabelle's neck and shoulders like some kind of sentient scarf. Jem was still trying to get her head around his appearance. Mirabelle interacted with him like a protective older sister. It was strange to see, but as someone with an older brother she understood that bond.

"This is the dining room," said Mirabelle, pushing her way through a polished set of double doors.

The room was taken up by a very long table. At the end of

it sat Bertram. He was surrounded by various bowls, plates, and silver platters, all filled with food. Once again Jem was struck by seeing so much food in one place.

Bertram tore some meat off the nearest plate as they walked toward him.

"Roast chicken," he cried. He gestured at the spread. "And peas and gravy and carrots and something called mash."

"Shouldn't you be asleep, Uncle?"

Bertram shook his head. "Too much excitement. Too much going on. Just look at this marvelous repast provided by Odd." He held a bowl up in one hand and tilted it toward her, almost shrieking with delight. "Look at this! This is *ice cream*."

He nodded enthusiastically at them and then frowned as he looked into the bowl. "Oh, it appears to have lost its solidity."

"I think it's melting," said Mirabelle.

Bertram quickly put the bowl down and wiped his hand on his jacket. He eyed the bowl nervously.

"Melting? Why would it do that?"

Jem was bemused by Bertram's seeming lack of basic knowledge. Mirabelle winked at her as if to say "just play along."

He carefully opened a notebook by his side, took a pencil from it, and licked the tip in preparation, all the time keeping his eyes on the bowl of ice cream as if he feared it might grow legs and make a dash for it. He gave a flourish with the pencil.

"I shall commence my preparatory notes. First I shall write down my visual and olfactory observations. Then the tasting shall begin."

"Why not try something a bit more daring, Uncle?" asked Mirabelle. "Why not attempt to *eat* the ice cream right now?" She looked at Jem with a twinkle in her eye. It was a small thing, but it made Jem feel trusted, part of something.

Bertram's cheek twitched. "Well, well . . . perhaps."

He reached for the bowl and brought it to his lips, smiling nervously at Mirabelle and Jem. He squeezed his eyes shut, then sipped hesitantly. He paused for a moment, sipped with a little more confidence, then put the bowl down with a satisfied "Ah."

"Interesting," he said as he started writing in his notebook.

Mirabelle whispered to Jem. "This is Uncle's latest hobby. He likes to record the taste of things. The thing is he can't actually taste human food, unless it's raw meat, but we like to humor him."

Gideon offered his judgment on the subject by sticking his tongue out and making a tiny "bleh" sound.

The doors were flung open, and in walked Aunt Eliza. Her jet-black hair was piled on top of her head and held with a diamond pin. She had changed into fresh clothes and was wearing an ankle-length scarlet dress that shimmered, and long white silk gloves. Around her neck she wore a purple feather boa. Jem was taken aback by her poise and grace.

Eliza scrunched up her face in distaste as she looked at what Bertram had in front of him.

"What is *that*?" she asked, her voice sounding thick with bile.

"This is roast chicken," said Bertram proudly. "And this is ice cream."

"How does it taste?" said Eliza, her nose wrinkled in disgust.

"Marvelous," said Bertram.

Aunt Eliza didn't look convinced. She settled herself into a chair and reclined casually with one knee over the other.

"You should be sleeping, Aunt," said Mirabelle.

Eliza puffed her cheeks out and exhaled. "Indeed, and I was about to retire and was commencing my beauty regime, but then I saw Daisy flapping by in my mirror again like some kind of panicked fish, and suddenly I just seemed to lose all interest."

Eliza's left cheek started to ripple. Jem blinked, not quite sure what she was seeing, but there was a definite movement, as if the older lady's skin were alive.

"Aunt," said Mirabelle, touching her own cheek by way of warning.

"Oh," said Eliza. She patted her cheek. "Hush now," she said softly, and her cheek became placid again.

Jem wanted to ask about what she'd just seen, but she felt

frozen to the spot by the strangeness of it all. Just when she thought she'd regained her balance and begun to adjust to this bizarre new world, something else would unsettle her.

"You look beautiful, Eliza," said Bertram, patting her on the arm.

"Why thank you, Bertram. How very kind."

Bertram grinned like a baby. "Not as beautiful as Rula, though." He bit into a carrot and gazed wistfully into the distance, chomping away, immune to its flavor. "Oh, Rula," he sighed.

Eliza shook her head and rolled her eyes at Mirabelle, who smiled in response.

"Let's go, Jem," said Mirabelle.

"Where to?" asked Eliza, her eyes narrowing, her tone surprisingly sharp.

Mirabelle beamed innocently at her. "Nowhere special, Aunt."

Both Eliza and Bertram exchanged a glance. Bertram in particular looked worried.

"You're not going anywhere you shouldn't, are you?" he said.

"Not down below," said Eliza. She fixed Mirabelle with a stern look. It was definitely not a question.

Bertram shook his head. "You can't go down there, not with her," he said, looking at Jem, his voice a terrified whisper.

"We can't, we shan't, we won't," said Mirabelle.

Her uncle and aunt looked at them both. Even Gideon's

ears were pricked as he paid attention. A definite air of disquiet had seeped into the room, and Jem suddenly felt uncomfortable with the attention.

Eliza eventually sighed and shook her head.

"You really do go to great lengths sometimes to annoy your uncle," she said.

Mirabelle was still smiling. "I'm just giving Jem a tour."

She grabbed Jem's arm, and they were back out in the hall before Jem had time to draw breath. Jem wanted to ask Mirabelle why her aunt and uncle seemed so uneasy with the idea of them going "down below," but Mirabelle was already dashing ahead. Jem followed, rounding a corner just in time to see Mirabelle vanish into another room. Jem tensed in preparation for what lay inside, but nothing could have prepared her for what came next.

The dozens of glowing lights were hard enough to take in, but it was the sheer volume of portraits that lined the walls, and the walls themselves seemingly stretching on and on into forever, that overwhelmed her. Jem's breath caught in her chest as she looked up and realized she couldn't see the ceiling.

It felt as if the floor had suddenly tilted, and she was finding it hard to stand up straight. Then Mirabelle's hand lightly took her elbow.

"This is the Room of Lights," said Mirabelle.

"There are so many of them," Jem managed to gasp.

She had never seen so many colors—blazing pinks,

muted golds, shimmering reds—all hanging in the air to form a burning tapestry.

"What are they?" Jem asked.

"Enoch calls them the Spheres. They're ways in to this world," said Mirabelle, smiling herself, as if she too were seeing the lights for the first time.

Ways in to this world. It seemed such a simple statement, but it set Jem's mind reeling again. *Ways in, but from where and for who or what?* She remembered Mirabelle's talk of a mirror realm. She found herself trying to put these strange new ideas into some kind of order.

"There are places throughout the world, hidden places like this house, where there are gateways between your world and the Ether. Uncle Enoch says that the House of Rookhaven has the largest number of these gateways."

Somehow Jem managed to peel her eyes away from the glowing orbs. Now she looked at the portraits. One large portrait featured a creature that looked like a rhino. It had a horn where a nose should have been, but its face was brown and leathery, and it had three golden eyes. Its shoulders were huge, and it was dressed in what looked like a glossy brown dressing gown made of some kind of animal fur.

"That's Uncle Alfred," said Mirabelle. "One of the older generation. One of those who lived abroad."

"Abroad?"

"In your world," said Mirabelle.

Jem frowned, wondering how a rhino in a fur

coat could live unseen in the outside world and how one could use the term "uncle" to describe it.

Two boys dressed in Edwardian tweed sat on a futon in another portrait. The boys were identical, right down to the arms that protruded from the sides of their heads.

"Quentin and Richard Haxley. Very well-respected members of the Family. Very old and wise. They liked to juggle. I'm told they were very popular at parties."

Jem's attention was now taken with a large, doughy-looking woman sitting on a bench. Two extremely tall spindly men stood on either side of her, each with a hand on her shoulder. All three had mouths and nostrils, but no eyes. The mouths were curved into smiles filled with pointed, razor-sharp teeth.

"Mavis Dibble and the Dibble twins. Notorious talkers and terrible gossips."

Mirabelle pointed at a painting of a young woman with three heads. Each head was identical except one had green eyes, one blue, and one brown. Their matching fierce gazes seemed to burn through the picture.

"Aunt Rula. She went traveling over a century ago. Uncle Bertram had a bit of a thing for her." Mirabelle frowned for a moment. "Well, for one of her heads, anyway. I think it was the middle one. The other two were rather jealous. He still pines after her, expecting her to come home some day." Mirabelle shrugged. "Perhaps she will."

Jem glanced at another painting. It was of something that looked like a black gloopy substance contained in a jar. The black gloopy substance had two blue eyes, both surprisingly beautiful and filled with an aching melancholy.

"Uncle Urg," said Mirabelle.

"Urg?" said Jem.

"Urg."

Jem started to laugh, Mirabelle joined in, and Gideon started chittering too. Suddenly a wave of dizziness washed over her, and she found it hard to breathe. The room seemed to be getting larger with each passing moment. She flapped her hand at Mirabelle, and Gideon tilted his head in curiosity, blinking his one eye as he regarded her.

Mirabelle took Jem back into the hall. Jem slumped against the wall and took a few deep breaths.

"It's a lot to take in," said Mirabelle sympathetically.

Jem nodded.

"Urg," she said.

"Urg," said Mirabelle, and the laughter started all over again.

Mirabelle took Jem to the fifth floor to a room at the corner of the house. Jem's legs were aching by the time they reached their destination. When Mirabelle opened the door, she flinched from the beams of sunlight that shone through the holes in the roof. A large window had been boarded up. The ceiling had been torn away, and the bare rafters holding up this section of the roof could be seen. Some were soggy and soft looking, presumably because of the rain that came in through the holes. About a dozen ravens were arranged along some of the beams. Jem was surprised by how eerily quiet they were, as if they were watching. The floor was covered in bird droppings and the occasional pool of water.

"This is the Room of Knives," said Mirabelle.

"Why is it called that?" asked Jem.

Mirabelle stepped toward one of the beams of sunlight. She circled it with her palms held up as if warming them. She pirouetted gracefully round another sunbeam and tiptoed between two more. Jem's heart thudded so hard as she watched this display that she could feel it pulsing in her mouth. She had to fight the urge to run across the room and grab Mirabelle. All she could think of was that scorched shadow outside the house. Gideon pressed himself closer to Mirabelle's neck, mewling nervously. Mirabelle shushed him.

"Because on a day like today it's filled with knives of sunlight," said Mirabelle. "One misstep and I could land in a sunbeam, then *poof*." She splayed her fingers out like a magician demonstrating a disappearing trick. "No more me."

"Be careful," said Jem.

A raven flew down, and Mirabelle put out her hand for it to land. "*Quawk quawk*," it said into her face, then it pivoted and stared at Jem with its one good eye. "*Quawk*," it said again, as if accusing her of something.

Mirabelle chuckled. "It's all right—Jem is a friend."

"*Quawk*," said Gideon, raising his head in defiance, causing Mirabelle to smile.

The raven dipped its head up and down vigorously for a few moments then flew back into the rafters, cawing at its companions and receiving muted caws in response as if they were all discussing the interloper.

As Mirabelle led her out of the room, Jem looked back up at the ravens in the rafters: the occasional flap here, a beak rubbing a wing there, but no other sound from them.

"My mum always said it was bad luck to let a bird into a room."

"These birds have always been here, and we've never had any bad luck," said Mirabelle.

Even so, Jem couldn't help looking up at them with a

certain mistrust. They looked as if they were waiting for something, but she didn't say this to Mirabelle for fear she might laugh at her.

Mirabelle brought Jem to a library next. Four levels of shelves were filled with dusty leather-bound books, and when Jem opened some of them, they were filled with runes from languages she'd never seen before.

They visited several more rooms, and soon it all became a blur. They took time for a snack in the now empty dining room. Mirabelle didn't eat a thing, despite the spread in front of them. Gideon peered down from her shoulder with a look of distaste. Jem ate a chicken sandwich while Mirabelle told her more about her family history. Jem listened with awe to stories so strange she could barely take them in. She was particularly intrigued when Mirabelle told her about the Ether.

"But what is it, and how do you . . ." She tried to think of the word. "Emerge from there?"

"The lights in the Room of Lights are the way in. Like gateways. That's how I came here. It's where we're all from," said Mirabelle. "Aunt Eliza tried to explain it to me once. She says no one knows exactly what the Ether is, but she likes to think of it as a place of souls, and the souls drift among each other, all of them waiting for their moment. And then when one is ready it crosses over into this world to become part of the Family."

"It's like being born," said Jem.

Mirabelle frowned. "Yes, I suppose it is."

"And there are more places like this? Are they hidden by magic too?"

Mirabelle nodded.

Through a chink in a curtain, Jem could see the sun was sinking low in the sky. As they finally left the dining room, Jem felt that with each step she was lurching from one strange dream into another.

Gideon leaped from Mirabelle's shoulders and then looked guiltily at her.

Mirabelle pointed a finger. "Remember now, Gideon, behave. No wandering off."

Gideon squeaked at her, then suddenly vanished into thin air. Jem blinked in disbelief.

"He found his talent quite quickly after he arrived in the house. He's been practicing," said Mirabelle.

There was the sound of something scampering away.

"There he goes," said Mirabelle, coming to a stop.

They were standing at the entrance to the corridor that led down toward the larder.

"It won't hurt just to look, despite what Aunt Eliza and Uncle Bertram say," said Mirabelle.

"So this is the way to 'down below'?" said Jem.

Mirabelle nodded.

That was when Jem heard it. A long, low moan rising up from the dark. She took an instinctive step back.

"Come on," said Mirabelle, looking completely unperturbed.

A slightly reluctant Jem followed her past the larder and into the dark. The floor sloped downward, and the air had a moist, earthy quality. The more they descended, the colder it got. Jem could feel the back of her neck tingling. Eventually they reached a long corridor gloomily lit by two dirty yellow bulbs set into wall sconces.

Mirabelle stopped before a huge iron door set into the wall. It looked completely out of place with its surroundings, and in the dim light Jem could make out dozens of strange figures in bas-relief on its surface. Things that looked like two-headed dragons fought with bellowing ogres with mouths like caves. A creature with the head of an eagle and the body of a lion was ripping into the shredded carcass of a giant serpent. On and on these figures went, filling almost every inch of the door.

One figure in particular caught her attention. A creature with long, bony limbs and claws with its skin hanging off. It seemed to be howling and attempting to devour everything around it. Looking at it made her uneasy.

Mirabelle laid a hand on the door, closed her eyes, and nodded to herself, her mouth moving as she said something under her breath. The air was getting colder and Jem shivered.

Mirabelle opened her eyes and smiled at her.

"That's done. I like to say hello."

Hello to whom? Jem wondered. She felt relieved when

they made their way back up the slope and headed toward the kitchen.

The kitchen was gray and dusty, and Jem thought it peculiar that a family with such a large dining room would have a kitchen that looked as if it hadn't been used in decades.

"Let me show you the garden," said Mirabelle.

She took a step toward the back door, then pulled up suddenly. The sun was setting behind the trees, and Mirabelle had a faraway look in her eyes.

"What is it?" asked Jem.

"I just need a moment. It's not safe yet," said Mirabelle without taking her eyes off the sun, her expression still dreamlike.

Jem turned to watch the sunset through the window: livid tongues of orange and red lit up a sky bruised to a deep, rich purple. They faded as the sun finally disappeared.

Mirabelle sagged, sighing with what seemed to be a mixture of relief and disappointment. She opened the back door and motioned Jem to step through.

It was warm in the garden. The night air hissed softly through the leaves. Jem could see enough to notice that the garden was overgrown, but there was a rightness to its wildness, a kind of pleasing symmetry to the chaos.

Mirabelle had deftly unhooked a bucket from beside the back door. Now she swung it back and forth, whistling as she went. Jem stopped abruptly when she saw what lay ahead. There was a huddled mass of flowers clumped together on a patch of grass. They were the same type of flowers that had attacked her and Tom. They were slightly smaller than their counterparts on the path, but there was no mistaking the thick stalks and drooping heads. They looked as if they were sleeping.

Mirabelle looked over her shoulder at Jem. "Come on. They won't bite. I won't let them."

Mirabelle held the bucket up so that Jem could see its contents. It was filled with bones. Some had a little meat and gristle still attached. "Flower food," Mirabelle said.

She took a bone out of the bucket and waved it almost serenely back and forth in the air. One of the flowers straightened up and unfurled its petals, then looked directly at Jem and hissed.

Jem had a strong urge to run, but felt a hand squeezing her arm. Mirabelle looked at her reassuringly.

"Don't be afraid. They won't hurt you. Not while I'm here."

Mirabelle threw a bone high above her head. It wheeled end over end, and as it arced toward the flowers, several more unfurled their petals with a soft peeling sound. As the bone made its descent, at least three of the flowers snapped at the air in an attempt to grab it. One was successful, and Jem watched in horrified fascination as the bone landed in what passed for a mouth. The flower sucked it down, while its companions shrieked and hissed in anger.

"Hush now!" Mirabelle shouted, taking a step toward them.

The flowers whipped
their necks about for a moment
before settling down, their heads bobbing gently as they
regarded Mirabelle.

Mirabelle held another bone out and urged one of the
flowers forward like someone coaxing a dog with a biscuit.
The flower leaned down and took it gently from Mirabelle,
then straightened up as it swallowed it back.

"These are a young batch. The Flowers of Divine Lapsidy
have been protecting the house for hundreds of years.
They do tend to wander a little, but they've made a solemn
promise never to go into the outside world."

Mirabelle handed Jem a chicken bone. "You try it."

Jem took the bone. She was keenly aware that several
of the flowers were now crowding against one another as
they jostled for position, vying for her attention. Jem tensed
herself and raised the bone toward the nearest flower. The
flower bowed its head and slowly took the bone between its
cupped petals, threw its head back, and gulped it down. Jem
was surprised when it started cooing, then dipped its head
toward her, as if bowing.

"Go on," said Mirabelle.

Jem reached out and touched the flower's petals. They felt like silk. The flower nuzzled her cheek and cooed some more while its companions chirruped and murmured, as if in appreciation.

"You see?" Mirabelle giggled. "Nothing to be afraid of."

Mirabelle scattered more bones around the flowers, and they proceeded to pick them up and eat them with a little more civility while Jem and Mirabelle sat watching from a nearby bench. There was a symphony of smacking, crunching, biting, and gentle hissing. Jem was utterly hypnotized by the scene. She shook her head in disbelief.

"What *is* this place?" she asked.

Mirabelle shrugged. "Home."

"But it's separate from everything . . . and you're all . . ."

Mirabelle tilted her head and waited.

"Different," said Jem, feeling as soon as she said the word that it was the wrong thing to say. She was relieved when Mirabelle threw her head back and laughed.

"We're people, like you. But not like you. We're—"

"Just people," said Jem, nodding in understanding.

"We're family," said Mirabelle.

"Why do you hide?"

Mirabelle started to swing her legs, looking at her shoes as she spoke. "Once, long ago, your people and ours didn't exactly see eye to eye. Some of us went out into the world when we emerged from the Ether, and your people hunted us." Mirabelle paused for a moment. She seemed to be considering something. "Many generations ago, we came to an agreement with humankind so that we could all live in peace. The agreement is called the Covenant."

"And the people in the village, have they always known about your existence?"

Mirabelle nodded. "Yes, the agreement was made with their ancestors and extends to the world beyond the village. Meanwhile we stay here, and they stay in the village, keeping our home a secret. Members of the Family can choose to wander into the outside world, but they can't reveal their true selves or do harm to any humans. Any members of the Family who wish to can return here whenever they want, like Odd coming and going. Uncle Enoch calls this place 'a pocket out of time.' It's contained both within and without your world because of magic that has been worked by those who came before. If you have the key, you can gain access." She made a face. "Or if the magic starts to wear thin and age, which is how you managed to get in."

Jem considered all this. There was so much to take in, but the idea of people appearing from globes of lights fascinated her most of all, even after everything else she'd seen.

"But don't you have parents?" she asked at last.

Mirabelle shook her head. "We have each other."

"But . . ." Jem trailed off. It just seemed so strange to her, the idea of emerging from some mysterious otherworld, and not having parents.

"What about you?" asked Mirabelle. "Do you have parents?"

A cold dagger between the shoulder blades would have been kinder, but Jem tried not to show her pain. She shook her head. It took an effort to finally speak.

"My dad died in the war, and Mum . . . my mum died afterward."

Jem turned her face away and felt the telltale prickling of tears at the corner of her eyes.

"I'm sorry," said Mirabelle.

Jem waved a hand as if there was nothing to be concerned about and tried to smile.

She could sense the hesitation in Mirabelle's voice when she asked her next question.

"What's it like? Losing someone, I mean. It's just that we don't age or die like you do, and . . ."

There was a long pause. A sudden great stillness. Even the flowers seemed to be listening.

"It hurts," said Jem, trying to focus on the flowers, who now seemed to be looking at her sympathetically.

"Where?" asked Mirabelle.

Jem looked at her. Mirabelle seemed genuinely at a loss. Her brow furrowed as if she was trying to translate a strange new language.

"Here," said Jem, laying a palm against her own chest. She thought about it for a moment. "Everywhere," she said, clenching her hands.

A soft silence descended again, eventually broken by a solitary word from Mirabelle.

"Sorry."

Jem looked at her and nodded.

"I didn't mean to upset you," said Mirabelle.

"You didn't," said Jem.

Mirabelle looked grateful.

They watched the flowers. Their meal finished, they now curled their petals inward and lowered their heads to sleep.

The garden was quiet. The two girls sat in silence, both of them feeling suddenly at home in the cavernous blue night that surrounded them.

When Jem got back to the bedroom she shared with Tom, she found him on the floor scrabbling under the bed. He pulled himself out from under it, looking slightly exasperated.

"Nothing," he said. "There's absolutely nothing here!"

"What are you doing? You should be in bed."

Tom stood up and dusted himself off. He picked up a candlestick from the blanket. "I did find this. What do you think it's worth?"

He held it out, and Jem frowned and pushed it aside. "Get back into bed."

He rolled his eyes and smiled, but the smile vanished as he was suddenly racked by a bout of coughing. Jem stepped toward him, but he raised a hand to stay her, and coughed a little more into his forearm.

"It's all right. I'm a lot better."

"Did you eat?"

"The big fellow brought me some dinner. He really likes to talk, doesn't he? Mainly about food. I reckon he's loaded. His clothes are a bit worn, but they were worth something once. I'll bet he's one of those who has all his dosh in a suitcase under his bed."

Tom walked over to the table, where some food was still laid out. He crammed bread into his mouth and talked with his mouth full.

"Where have you been all day?"

"Mirabelle was showing me around."

"Did you see those flowers and that bear again? I wonder what this place is exactly. It's like some elaborate parlor trick."

Jem shook her head. "It's no parlor trick. And there are other things, unusual things."

"More unusual than man-eating flowers?"

Jem didn't know what to say. It was hard to put into words exactly what she'd seen. She fully expected to be laughed at.

"It's a big house," she said. "There's a lot to explain. Maybe later when I've had time to think."

Tom froze midswallow, his eyes wide. "Did you see anything valuable?"

Jem shook her head angrily. "No, Tom. Not this time. We're guests."

Tom advanced toward her. "Go on, Jem. Tell me."

"You're not stealing anything," said Jem, standing her ground. She didn't like the look in Tom's eyes. That all-too-familiar wild light, the slightly crazed, almost hungry look, barely masking the desperation and the hurt. That hurt came bubbling to the surface now.

"Have you seen this place?" he said, gesturing around him. "It's huge. No one who has nothing has a house like this. They're hiding something. Whatever they have, they're hiding it. I bet they've got more stuff than the stinking Allisons!"

His face was contorted and ugly when he said that name. The Allisons were a rich local family who had employed their mum as a secretary for years. When she got sick, the Allisons had simply let her go. They never sent her anything. They never asked after her. When she died, only Tom and Jem were at her funeral. Afterward they would see old Mr. Allison with his finely coiffured silver hair being driven around town by his chauffeur, nose in the air, the look of a man who didn't have to deal with the paltry things in life.

His car had been burned out months later. No one knew who did it, apart from Jem, and she never spoke to Tom about it.

"Think of it, Jem," Tom said now, nodding furiously as if that alone might persuade her. "Think of all the stuff they have here."

"They have nothing," said Jem. "And even if they did, we're their guests."

Tom wheeled away from her in disgust. He leaned against the table and started cramming grapes into his mouth.

"They have plenty," he said sulkily. "Look at this. They don't even have to worry about rationing. They've got all this food. More than they need."

"Whatever else they have, we have no right to take it."

Tom looked at her. "You weren't saying that when we robbed that butcher's in Fulham a few months back."

Jem felt the heat as her cheeks became pink.

"Or that time when we snaffled those pies from that shop on Denmark Street."

"This is different."

"How?"

Because I have a friend now, thought Jem. *I have a real friend. Someone strange, but someone nice. Someone who trusts me, and I trust her.*

She thought these things, but didn't say them. To say them

might invite Tom's derision. Even thinking them made her feel exposed, yet also stronger than she'd felt in a long time. It was a jumble of emotions she just couldn't tease out. She decided the best thing was to explain nothing.

"It just is," said Jem, feeling slightly foolish. She hated feeling like that, as if Tom somehow was in the right and she wasn't.

Tom coughed again.

"You need to get back into bed," said Jem.

Tom scowled, but he didn't resist when she took him by the elbow and led him over to the bed. She spotted the medicine bottle on his bedside locker.

"Have you been taking your medicine?"

"Yes," he said, his tone surly.

He clambered into bed.

"You should take some more," said Jem, unscrewing the bottle and pouring out a spoonful.

"It makes me drowsy," Tom complained.

Jem held the spoon toward him. Tom rolled his eyes, but he let her put the spoon in his mouth.

"Do you want me to fluff up your pillow?" she said.

Tom scowled again, but she could see him trying to fight a smile. He settled back and closed his eyes.

Jem was ravenous. She sat at the table and had some food while Tom drifted off. She ate a peach and some grapes, and followed that with a bacon sandwich and some ginger ale. She'd never tasted food like it. Years of rationing and being fed scraps by her uncle meant she'd never had anything this delicious before. It was heavenly. She was just finishing up when her attention was drawn to the door. She thought she heard something. A sound like someone whispering outside.

For a moment she couldn't move. Her heart started to pound, but she took some deep breaths to calm herself and then went to the door.

She reached out and turned the handle slowly.

The door opened. It was dark in the hallway, but it was also empty. Jem let out a sigh of relief.

"You shouldn't be out here," said a voice on the air.

Jem flinched.

"It's not safe. You should stay in your room."

Jem could barely move. Her heart thudded again, beating faster and faster.

She somehow found the strength to edge back into the room and slam the door shut behind her.

She lay against it for a moment, panting and trembling, trying to calm herself. She almost hopped out of her skin when she heard another voice.

"Something nice and tasteful. That's all I'm asking."

She looked at the bed where Tom lay with his eyes closed and a half smile on his face. He was clasping the candlestick gently against his chest.

"Just something nice . . . ," he murmured.

His features slackened as he fell into a deeper sleep.

Jem exhaled again.

She was still trembling slightly when she climbed under the blanket a few moments later to go to sleep. She was thinking about that voice she'd heard outside the room. Although she hadn't *heard* it exactly. Instead it had felt as if the voice had somehow invaded her mind. But there had been no one in the hallway. Only a solitary spider hanging from the ceiling just above her head.

Though she could have sworn it was looking right at her.

Mirabelle

"I showed her around," said Mirabelle.

She was standing in Uncle Enoch's study with her arms folded. Enoch was sitting behind his desk perusing some papers covered in arcane symbols and runes. He leaned back in his chair, closed his eyes for a moment, and rubbed the bridge of his nose between thumb and forefinger.

"Really? How very kind of you, Mirabelle."

Mirabelle stuck her chin out defiantly.

"I showed her everywhere. I showed her the Room of Lights. I took her to feed the flowers. I even showed her the Room of Knives. I told her all about the Family."

Enoch sighed. "Mirabelle, I have quite a bit of work to do concerning the Glamour, and this—"

"They're not from the village, but that doesn't mean we should turn our backs on them. We shouldn't turn our backs on anybody who needs our help. And *nobody* should have to put up with the likes of Daisy."

She stopped talking because Enoch was staring at her now, a curious expression on his face.

He stood up slowly and went to the window and looked out with his hands clasped behind his back. A moment passed. Mirabelle could feel the tension and silence begin to swell, until finally Enoch spoke.

"You're right, you know; we shouldn't turn anyone away."

Mirabelle wasn't sure what to say. She'd expected Enoch to be enraged, even hoped he'd be angry, but his muted response completely flummoxed her. Enoch kept looking out the window.

"I'll be going to dinner soon. I need to get some reading done before then."

"Yes, Uncle," said Mirabelle, knowing she was dismissed, but feeling a strange sense of loss now that her fury was dissipating.

As she turned to go, he spoke again.

"So you told her *everything* about us?"

"Yes."

"Did you tell her that her kind used to hunt us?"

"Yes."

"And that we used to hunt them too?"

Mirabelle bit her lip.

"No," she said quietly, looking at the floor.

"Mirabelle."

The sound of the pendant hitting the desk caught her attention. Enoch had already turned back to the window. Mirabelle picked up the pendant.

"Thank you, Uncle."

Enoch merely nodded.

Mirabelle walked into the hallway and closed the door behind her. She was still confused by her uncle's reaction. She'd expected him to explode with anger after her confession, and she certainly hadn't expected to get her pendant back. She also felt a twinge of guilt over not having told Jem the full family history.

A mirror shimmered on the wall to her left, glowing with a gray, nebulous fog that brightened to a sparkling whiteness as Odd's head popped out of it.

"Hello," he said, grinning at her. Then he frowned as if suddenly remembering something. "Hold on, just give me a sec."

His head disappeared back into the mirror, reappearing a moment later as he clambered out. He climbed down using the frame of the mirror as a handhold. When he had his feet on the ground, he shoved his hand under the mirror's surface, felt around for a bit, then pulled.

Daisy came flying out and hit the floor in an ungainly tangle of limbs. She jumped up, looking furious as she smoothed her pinafore and fixed her hair. She then stomped off down the hallway, glaring at Mirabelle as she passed her.

"You're welcome," Odd shouted after her.

"You'll be sorry," Daisy growled, wheeling back round to glare at Mirabelle again.

"I *am* sorry," said Mirabelle.

"You will be," Daisy snarled, disappearing round a corner.

"I am!" Mirabelle shouted.

Odd looked amused. "Was that an apology?"

"No. Yes. Maybe. I don't know," Mirabelle snapped.

Some items had dropped out of Odd's pocket as he

clambered through the mirror. There was a marble, the arrowhead he'd shown her previously, and the gold chain necklace again. He looked sheepish as he picked them all up and put them back in his pocket.

He nodded at her hand. "I see you got your pendant back."

"Enoch gave it to me."

Odd frowned. "Really?"

"Yes."

"That was rather forgiving of him."

Mirabelle wanted to say that she was surprised, that Enoch was acting strange, and that she'd expected something else from him. Anger perhaps. Rage. But she had recognized something in him. Something she'd seen today in the human girl, Jem, but only rarely in one of the Family. Enoch seemed sad.

"Do you think something's wrong with Enoch?" Mirabelle asked.

Odd looked slightly taken aback. "What?"

"Do you think he seems . . . I don't know . . . sad?"

Odd licked his lips and considered the question.

"Sad?"

"Yes."

"Well, I suppose he might have something to be sad about. Maybe he's finally come to terms with the fact that he's a little too full of his own self-importance. Perhaps he's beginning to bore himself to death with his ideas of tradition and—"

"Odd, please. Be serious for once."

Odd chuckled and avoided looking directly at her.

"Odd?"

Odd shook his head. "It's probably just the tear in the Glamour. It's a concern for him. That's all."

He looked at her now, and he was smiling, but Mirabelle got the sense that the smile was little more than a mask and that if she waited a moment longer it would crack.

"I really have to go now, Mirabelle."

Mirabelle nodded. "Don't go too far."

"I won't. Maybe I'll just take a quick jaunt to Mongolia."

"Aren't you going to the feast tonight?"

Odd patted his stomach. "I've already eaten."

He winked at her, then stepped quickly into a portal that had appeared behind him. The portal popped out of existence.

Mirabelle was left alone in the hallway, an afterimage of Odd's pale face playing in front of her. He'd seemed happy enough until she'd brought up the subject of how Enoch was feeling. Something about his reluctance to talk about it made her suspicious.

And there was no mistaking the brief look of relief on his face just before the portal had disappeared.

Piglet

A stillness lies over the house now. Piglet can feel it. But it is a stillness like a bowstring that has been wound too tight. Very soon it will snap.

When it does, Piglet knows that everything will be changed.

Changed forever.

Jem

Jem was woken by a noise in the dark.

It sounded like a soft thumping, and she lay there clutching the blanket while she waited and listened.

The sound didn't come again, and Jem started to relax. She could feel her pulse returning to normal, and she was about to turn over on the couch when she realized something was missing.

She listened hard again and knew exactly what it was.

The sound of another person breathing in the dark.

Jem threw off the blanket, leaped off the couch, and ran toward the bed. Her eyes were still adjusting to the dark, so she thrust her hands out to feel for her brother.

Tom was gone.

She knew exactly what he'd be up to. She scrabbled around on the floor for her shoes and socks, afraid to put the light on in case it attracted attention. She threw on her cardigan. Her heart pounded in her ears, and she tried to steady herself as she stepped out of the room.

The house was as dark and quiet as ever when she crept down the hallway. Her breath caught in her throat when she saw a clock on the wall that read two in the morning. She half expected to hear the voice she'd heard earlier outside the bedroom door.

Jem crept downstairs. She was wary of the fact that the stairs opened onto the main vestibule, and she was worried that someone or *something* might pass by and see her.

As she came closer to the dining room door, she thought she heard a noise. It sounded like something scraping against metal. Jem listened closely, holding her breath.

There was a flicker of light, orange and wisp-like, at the edge of the door.

She exhaled slowly. Waited. Listened.

The wind gave a low moan outside.

She heard the clink of something metallic and knew instinctively that it was Tom. Tom, who liked bright, shiny things and collecting candlesticks and clocks and ornaments to sell in pursuit of his dream of living in a fancy house. She could picture him behind the door, stealing as much as he could, just as he had done so often in other houses the length and breadth of the country even as she begged him not to.

Jem relaxed a little, but felt a twinge of anger.

She had to stop him. They were guests, after all. She thought of Mirabelle and felt a wave of shame.

She grabbed the handle and shoved the door open, ready to catch Tom in the act.

She hadn't expected to be greeted with a bloodcurdling howl.

Or by the sight of the horrific candlelit tableau before her.

The room was filled with monsters, and most of them

were eating from a long metal trough that stretched almost the length of the table. The enormous bear she and Tom had encountered before pulled its head from the trough and turned to her, baring its yellow teeth, ruby eyes burning with rage as it bellowed at her. Flecks of blood sprayed from its lips and landed on the wooden floor. A writhing black shape twisted beside the bear, its form changing and rippling from one moment to the next as it too bent over the trough. It straightened up, and Jem saw the center of its head fizz with sudden movement as if its very essence was being sucked into a whirlpool, and she felt her gorge rise as she realized a face was forming.

The howling continued for a few moments, and tumbling into the room, she saw the source of the sound. Two small creatures were dressed in the twins' clothes. Their faces were gnarled and twisted, their eyes black and shining. They had yellow fangs. They both clung to the large bone they'd obviously been fighting over before Jem entered the room.

You shouldn't be here, a voice shouted in her mind, and she recognized it as the voice from earlier that evening. Something else was familiar about it, but she couldn't think what. She so wanted to run, but fear gripped her hard, and she couldn't move.

The cold gust of air caused by the shadow that rose up from the back of the room broke her paralysis.

Jem ran.

She reached the main hallway and raced toward the front door. Her thoughts were wild, panicked, and scattered, like leaves in a storm. She grabbed the handle and twisted it.

The door was locked.

Jem pounded on it.

She could feel movement behind her.

She turned.

The creatures were coming toward her. The bear was snapping its jaws and snarling. The two girls were hissing and clawing the air. She saw the lump of dark matter convulsing as it tried to render itself into a recognizable human shape while dragging a dress behind it.

Jem expected the monsters to fall on her. She didn't expect them to part and make way for the shadow that loped toward her now, wings extended, gnashing its teeth and shrieking at her.

She looked into its face, into its dark eyes, its long incisors. Jem's legs almost buckled as it lunged toward her.

"Enoch! No!"

Jem felt a mixture of terror and relief as Mirabelle appeared in front of her, swiftly interposing herself between Jem and the bat-like creature.

Enoch, she said Enoch, Jem thought, her mind a flurry as she looked from Mirabelle to the creature.

The monster snarled at Mirabelle, but Mirabelle stepped toward it, her jaw jutting forward defiantly.

"Leave her alone!"

The creature gave a great flap of its wings and the air cracked. It threw up a gust of wind so strong that Jem was almost knocked off her feet.

Mirabelle, to her credit, stood ramrod straight before it, her fists clenched.

"I said, Leave her alone."

The monster's eyes went from Jem to Mirabelle, and amazingly its wings started to fold in on themselves. Its features began to flow and smooth to a pale whiteness,

and everything changed,
except for its eyes, which
remained completely black and
pitiless. It raised its head in a familiar
aloof way, and there was no mistaking
the grim face of Uncle Enoch as he
glared down at her.

"She disturbed the sacred feast,"
he snarled at Mirabelle.

Some of the creatures behind
him growled in agreement.

"How was she to know?" Mirabelle shouted at them.

"She should show some re-
spect!" Enoch roared.

The black, undulating shape began to flow
toward them from the back of the hallway. It
made a sound like sand in a gigantic hourglass as
the spiders that made up the constituent parts
of its body began to flow together and form a
familiar shape.

"Aunt Eliza," Jem gasped. Now she understood why the
voice she'd heard earlier had sounded so familiar.

Eliza's face was half-formed. Hundreds of spiders were
rushing together across the floor and joined their fellows
as they raced upward to form the body that now filled the
gown they'd been dragging.

Eliza put a restraining hand on Enoch's arm, and Jem could see the agitation of the spiders as they spun in dark lines and settled together to form her limbs. "Enoch, please. She wasn't to know."

Enoch trembled with fury as he looked down at Mirabelle and Jem. The bear shambled to and fro behind him, while the twins licked their teeth and stared hungrily at Jem.

Enoch was about to say something when a hideous shriek came from the bowels of the house. It was the howling of someone in utter agony. Jem recognized it instantly.

"Tom!" she screamed.

Piglet

Piglet is surprised when the door opens. It hasn't been opened in a very, very long time.

He is even more surprised when he sees the boy standing there, mouth agape.

The boy is new. When the boy looks up at him, Piglet can see the terror in his eyes.

"Oh no, no," the boy says, his voice catching in his throat. And Piglet tilts his head and wonders what might have frightened him so.

The boy backs away, but it seems as if he has forgotten how to use his legs, and he stutters and stumbles backward, falling to the floor.

"No, please," he moans.

Piglet feels something. He feels . . .

He has to think about this.

Piglet feels sorry for him.

Piglet knows that the boy is not simply terrified now; the fact is the boy is terrified all the time. Piglet can see it in his green eyes, and in the lines that have appeared on a face that is much too young for them. Piglet sighs in compassion.

But Piglet is also hungry.
Oh, so very hungry.
And the door is open.

There is only one thing to do.
And when he does it, the boy screams.

Mirabelle

Mirabelle had instinctively grabbed Jem's hand, and they'd both dashed into the deepest part of the house with the others in hot pursuit. She had never seen Piglet's door open before, but here it stood now, swinging on its great brass hinges, a soft murmurous breeze emanating from the cool interior, the scent of damp earth wafting from the centuries-old blackness, and a large skeleton key angled awkwardly in the lock.

The stunned silence felt like nails across Mirabelle's soul. Bertram had reverted to his human aspect and was leaning against the wall, inconsolable, as tears streamed down his face. Both Dotty and Daisy were clutching each other and weeping. Even Gideon had heard the commotion and was rocking fretfully back and forth in the dark behind them.

A frozen Enoch blinked rapidly for a few moments, while Eliza placed a gentle hand on his arm, her other hand covering her mouth in shock.

Jem broke the silence.

"Where is he? Where's Tom?"

She was white-faced, frantic. Mirabelle didn't know what to say to her.

"We should close it," Enoch said quietly.

Bertram laughed bitterly through his tears. "It's a bit late for that now, isn't it?"

Jem stood in front of Enoch. "Where is he? What's happened to my brother?"

Mirabelle felt a fierce stab of pride as she watched her friend confront Enoch.

Enoch tilted his head and looked at Jem as if he'd come across a strange specimen of flower and wasn't quite sure what to make of it. His expression was almost one of pity. Mirabelle wanted to slap him.

Enoch shook his head. "Piglet is free. You have no idea what that means."

"Where is he? Where's Tom?" Jem screamed.

Enoch turned away from her and gestured toward the open door. Dotty and Daisy stepped forward and pushed the door closed. It slammed shut with a great iron *clang*.

"Where is my brother?" Jem pleaded, grabbing Mirabelle's arm.

Eliza pointed toward the other end of the corridor. "There's a door that way. It leads up and out."

"Don't worry. We'll find him. He'll be fine," said Mirabelle, trying her best to sound reassuring and hoping her eyes didn't betray her fear.

She turned to Enoch.

"We have to find Piglet."

Bertram whimpered, and Enoch shook his head. "I won't allow it. Confronting Piglet would be too risky for any of us. We must stay here within the confines of the estate."

Mirabelle spluttered in disbelief. "We can't just let him escape. We have to find him and bring him back!"

"But Piglet is dangerous," Bertram moaned, cramming his knuckles against his mouth.

"Bertram is correct," said Eliza.

Mirabelle couldn't believe what she was hearing. She looked from one to another, and each of them looked terrified, even Eliza. She was so angry now that there was a whooshing sound in her ears.

"He can't be allowed to roam free. He *can't*."

Enoch closed his eyes and sighed. "Mirabelle, you need to understand . . ."

Mirabelle stepped toward Enoch. "You're afraid of him," she growled.

Enoch looked as if he'd been slapped.

Mirabelle grabbed Jem's hand. "We're going to find Tom and Piglet and bring them both back."

"You will do no such thing!" Enoch shouted.

Mirabelle gave an angry, defiant smile. "Oh yes we will."

"Mirabelle, you can't," Eliza pleaded.

"She can and she will," said a voice behind Mirabelle.

Odd stepped from the shadows, and Mirabelle felt the sudden urge to run and hug him.

Odd fixed Enoch with a determined look. "She'll find them."

Enoch looked unconvinced. "And how, pray tell, will she accomplish this if she can't leave the grounds?"

Odd gave a dismissive shrug. His hands were clasped behind his back. "She'll leave. She just won't do it through the front door."

Odd was making circles in the air with the little finger of his right hand. Mirabelle grabbed Jem just as she felt the cold air behind her. She saw Enoch's eyes widen as he looked over her shoulder, saw the look of determination on Odd's face as he wheeled round and pushed both her and Jem through the portal that had formed behind them.

There was a sudden popping sound, and the sensation of being squeezed through a tiny gap, and Mirabelle felt herself propelled forward at impossible speed . . .

She gasped, and her lungs filled with cold night air. She was surrounded by trees, and the night sky above her was sprinkled with stars. She tottered backward as if she'd been kicked, but she felt Odd's hands on her arms as he steadied her.

"Give it a minute." He led her toward a tree against which Jem was already leaning.

Jem was gasping too and looking up at the sky. "What just happened?" she asked.

Odd shrugged as if it were nothing. "We left the house."

"Where is it?" asked Mirabelle, looking around to get her bearings.

Odd licked the tip of his finger and held it up in the

air and frowned. "About half a mile back that way," he said, pointing behind him.

"Odd, you let us travel with you," said Mirabelle, shocked.

Odd looked at the ground. "Well, you needed help."

Mirabelle touched his arm. "But you never let anyone travel with you. 'No one goes with Odd.' That's what you always say."

Odd lifted his head and smiled awkwardly.

"Tom? What's happened to Tom?" Jem wailed.

"I think Piglet took him," said Mirabelle. "But we'll find him. I promise."

Mirabelle tried to smile encouragingly, but the look of fear on Jem's face only increased her own. She tried to tamp it down.

"Come on," Odd said. "I think Piglet's gone that way."

Mirabelle and Jem followed him in the dark. They walked for some time back in the direction of the house. Odd explained that Piglet could only have gone so far and that he had deliberately (he hoped) jumped ahead of him quite some distance beyond the Glamour. He led them to a small road with fields on one side and forest on the other. The earth beneath their feet was hard. The night was cold, and Jem was rubbing her upper arms vigorously even though she had her cardigan on. Odd gallantly took off his jacket and gave it to her. Jem nodded her thanks, and they continued on their way.

Mirabelle listened hard, but she couldn't detect a sound.

Then Odd stopped suddenly and bent down to inspect something at his feet.

They huddled around him. Jem spotted the dark liquid patch on the ground.

"It's nothing," Mirabelle said, trying not to show how frightened she was.

"It's blood," said Odd.

Mirabelle could have punched him.

Jem grabbed her. "He can't . . . It isn't . . ."

Mirabelle shushed her and shook her head. "It isn't."

"It definitely isn't," said Odd, sucking blood from the tip of a finger. He narrowed his eyes and looked at the field, and that's when they saw the clumped, fretful shadows lowing anxiously by the trees at the far side of the field. As Odd moved toward them, the shadows scattered, hooves rumbling in the dark, the panicked lowing getting louder.

"Cows," Odd said.

He came upon the ruin of a gate, a splintered, shattered tumble of planks, and then all their heads whipped round as they heard what sounded like a scream on the road up ahead.

Jem was gone before Mirabelle knew what was happening. She pounded up the rough path after her, shouting her name, but Jem wasn't listening. Mirabelle turned back to look for Odd, but he'd vanished.

There was another strangled howl. Mirabelle heard Jem shout Tom's name and watched her plunge into the trees.

Mirabelle followed her into the forest. She slapped low-hanging branches and bushes aside and finally broke into a clearing.

The first thing she saw was Odd and Jem by a tree. Tom was propped against it. His shirt was covered in something dark.

"It's blood!" Jem wailed.

The panic Mirabelle felt was all-consuming, but it was just for an instant because Odd said:

"It's all right—it's not his blood."

Then Tom's eyes flickered open, and he gave a weak smile.

Jem embraced him tightly, and he patted her on the back with a floppy hand.

"Jem," he gasped. His face twitched, and his eyes were wide and manic. He started to paw his sister's arms, as if he couldn't quite believe she was there. He tapped the side of his head. "He was in here. He saw everything."

Jem gasped as Tom squeezed her arms tightly. He was panting and babbling. Sweat was pouring down his face.

"There was Mum and Dad and me and you. And he looked at us and watched it all. And he, he . . ." Tom rocked back and forth and looked frantically about as if he'd lost something. He looked again at Jem, his eyes bulging. "He sees everything!" he wailed. Then his face crumpled, and he burst into tears.

"Who? Who sees everything?" Jem cried with a mixture of joy and terror.

Tom looked over her shoulder, but really it was the grunting snuffling that caught their attention.

And it was the rending, splintering sound that made them all turn.

For the first time in her life, Mirabelle laid her eyes upon Piglet.

And what a sight he was.

He was bent over the corpse of a cow, its shattered ribs jabbing upward into the night, steam rising from its entrails. It rocked back and forth as Piglet buried his snout in its innards and ripped and tore and rent and chewed and swallowed.

Piglet was as large as an elephant, then somehow as small as a dog. Then he expanded again, hulking over his prey, blotting out the stars. Looking at him was like trying to catch sight of the colors of a butterfly's wings in flight. Piglet seemed to change and run like paint in water, even as she looked upon him and came to a decision as to what he really looked like. One moment he was all eyes, dozens, perhaps hundreds, all blinking, all yellow, then he was all fangs, a gaping maw filled with scythe-like teeth, huge and impossibly sharp. He was claws and nails, ripping and tearing, his head horned and spiked, a ruffle of feathers round his neck. He was gold, then scarlet, his body shimmering like the fantail of a peacock. He sniffed and moaned with pleasure as he ate, and it seemed as if nothing else existed for him.

But he raised his head when Jem shouted at him.

"What did you do to him?"

Mirabelle had been so rapt by the sight of Piglet that she hadn't even noticed Jem advancing toward him. She tried to grab her, but Jem shrugged her arm away.

"What did you do to him?" she screamed, her whole body trembling with rage.

Piglet raised his head and sniffed the air. His eyes narrowed. They were green now, or were they red, flecked with a molten gold?

He threw back his head and bellowed.

Then it was Mirabelle's turn to scream as Piglet charged toward Jem.

Jem was rooted to the spot. Even the reliably instinctive Odd didn't seem to know what to do.

Mirabelle didn't think twice. She pushed Jem out of the way.

Piglet's form contracted and narrowed to a point, and now he was a spear of white light, and that spear hit Mirabelle full in the chest.

For Mirabelle everything seemed to freeze. Then there was the sensation of the world collapsing around her, and she felt as if she'd been swallowed by a tidal wave.

Mirabelle opened her eyes and found herself surrounded by mist, lilac in color, with little sunbursts of golden light flaring in it occasionally. She was transfixed by these tiny explosions, sometimes with figures in them, sometimes with places. She could see their outlines, their shapes. Some were more vivid than others.

She panicked for a moment, flailing like someone who has just fallen into deep water. Somehow she managed to calm herself simply by gazing at the images. The gold, the lilac, the explosions of color and light.

This is what Piglet sees, she thought.

And then she felt a sudden rush as another mind touched hers, and that mind was vast and old, and yet also terribly young, like that of a child.

"Piglet," she said in recognition, her voice echoing in the mist, tears of happiness springing to her eyes.

She knew him now. Knew him like never before, and he knew her. And she saw what he saw, and she saw . . .

The most recent thing Piglet had seen.

Tom and Jem standing by a grave, holding hands, their heads bowed. Mirabelle could feel Tom's pain. It was a raw thing that seemed to rake hot, burning furrows of agony even in her own mind, and she could feel his desperation and his sadness and his fear, and it was so overwhelming that she could feel herself choking on it.

The image ran and dissolved, like a watercolor in a rainstorm. Now Tom and Jem were sitting at a table, picking at a meager dinner. A hulking figure entered the room. He shouted something at them. Tom stood up and stepped between the figure and Jem. The man shouted some more. Then he raised a stick . . .

The image darkened, became a low, mean-looking house on a derelict street. Tom and Jem were creeping out of the front door, both of them carrying small bags. As they ran down the street, Mirabelle could almost taste their terror, mingled with a strange, desperate joy.

The picture changed. Tom and Jem were now in a room in an abandoned bombed-out house. Tom was shoving ration books into a rucksack. Jem was pleading with him to stop, and Mirabelle could feel his anger and fear and his . . .

The picture changed again. Tom crouched in a corner watching Jem sleep on a dingy mattress, clasping his knees tight to his chest, trying his best to muffle his sobs. Mirabelle knew his thoughts. And his guilt was a terrible, awful thing that loomed over him, ready to devour him, but he owed it to his parents to do everything, anything to save Jem. It was up to him now. Everything came down to him.

Mirabelle felt all this, knew all this, in an instant, as if Tom's very soul had been mapped out for her.

Another rushing sensation took her, as if she were being carried by a fast-moving current.

She was outside the House of Rookhaven now. But these were Piglet's memories, not Tom's.

The sky was gray; a soft wind blew. A car was coming up the driveway. She recognized it as Dr. Ellenby's. He parked in front of the house, stepped out of the car, and held the passenger door open for his companion. It was a woman. Dr. Ellenby took her hand as he helped her out. The woman clasped a hand to her round belly, pushed a strand of dark hair out of her eyes.

Enoch appeared at the front door, and Piglet tried and failed to decipher the look on his face. Mirabelle could sense his confusion. She concentrated on Enoch's face, to see whether she could read it herself, but she couldn't see clearly, and it was too late because the picture was already changing . . .

To a large bedroom. One that Mirabelle had seen before,

that she knew was part of the house. The woman was lying in the bed, and Dr. Ellenby had his shirtsleeves rolled up and was mopping her brow as the woman's head twisted and turned. Mirabelle noticed now how much younger Dr. Ellenby looked. His beard was darker, and he was saying something to the woman, smiling in that easy way of his, exuding the same warmth and sense of strength he always seemed to have.

Enoch was standing in the corner, looking at the floor, clasping his arms to his chest as if to comfort himself. For the first time in her vision Mirabelle perceived sound.

The woman screamed.

Piglet screamed.

Mirabelle screamed.

Silence and darkness descended.

There was nothing now, for what seemed like an eternity and an instant.

Nothing.

Then the silence was broken by the soft steady rhythm of a heartbeat. And somehow Mirabelle could sense that the heart was new.

The darkness started to dissipate, and now it was night, and Enoch was standing by the window looking out over the garden, and in his arms he held a baby swaddled in a blanket, and Enoch was . . . he was . . .

Mirabelle opened her eyes. She was vaguely aware that her forehead was pressed into the ground. She could smell soil and damp grass, and she gasped like someone coming up for air and raised herself onto her knees.

She looked around, and the world gradually came back into focus.

Jem and Odd were standing over her. Jem laid a hand on her shoulder; her lip was quivering.

"Mirabelle?"

Mirabelle tried to speak, but no words came out.

She looked woozily at Tom, who still sat with his back against the tree.

Tom smiled at her, but his eyes glittered with tears.

"I told you," he said. "I told you, didn't I?"

Mirabelle could only nod. She became aware that she was cradling something in the crook of her arm. It was dark and furry and small, and it mewled softly.

"What is it?" asked Jem.

A shaken Mirabelle finally found her words.

"This is Piglet," she said. She thought about it for a moment, realizing that he could still change shape at any moment. "For now," she added, her voice trembling.

Jem

It was the strangely sedate way everyone acted that confused Jem. Mirabelle seemed oddly calm as she cradled the creature in the crook of her arm.

She stumbled when she tried to stand, and both Odd and Jem had to grab an arm to steady her. Mirabelle looked at them, grateful, but also with an expression that suggested she was close to tears. Since she'd first met Mirabelle, the thing that Jem liked most about her was her serenity and confidence. Now, much like Tom, she seemed different somehow. It was this that frightened Jem more than anything. More than seeing Tom covered in blood. More than seeing the creature they called Piglet change its appearance with each passing moment. The same creature that had charged her seconds ago was now purring contentedly as it nestled into Mirabelle's chest.

"Piglet," Mirabelle whispered. She smiled down at him, then turned to Odd, her smile vanishing.

"Did you know?" she said, her face a rictus of rage.

Odd tried to meet her gaze, but it was so fierce that he looked at his feet. "Mirabelle . . . please—"

"Did you know, Odd?" Mirabelle roared.

Odd looked stricken. He took half a step toward Mirabelle, but she retreated and hugged Piglet closer.

Her eyes were fixed on Odd. Jem had no idea what was going on.

"We need to put him back in his room," said Odd, nodding at Piglet. "Let me help."

Odd started to make a circle in the air with his finger. Mirabelle grabbed his wrist and pushed his arm down viciously. Jem was shocked by the angry gesture.

"No!"

Odd blinked at her. He opened his mouth as if to say something, then he looked from Jem to Mirabelle and back again, as if seeking direction. He looked completely bereft. Jem felt a sudden sympathy for him.

"You need to go," said Mirabelle, her voice lower but no less angry.

Odd turned away from them, his head bowed, and vanished into a portal.

Jem helped Tom to his feet and put her arm round him, careful to avoid the blood on his shirt.

"I'm sorry, Jem," he said, his eyes brimming with tears.

"It's all right," she said.

"He was inside my head. He made me run out of the house. I couldn't stop him." He squeezed her arm so tight that Jem had to grit her teeth. "He sees everything, Jem. He hears everything. And he's so old. He's older than anything."

To calm him Jem smiled and nodded as if she understood what he meant. She hugged him fiercely to her with one arm as they made their way over to where Mirabelle stood.

"We have to get Piglet back to his room," Mirabelle said, looking as if she were barely keeping herself together. Jem could see the anger in her eyes, and the grief that lay beneath the surface. A grief so profound that Jem feared it might crack Mirabelle's alabaster skin.

Jem touched her arm tenderly. "What happened?" she whispered, for fear of waking Piglet.

Mirabelle shook her head and looked away for a moment.

"Piglet showed me things. Things that have been kept from me," she replied hoarsely.

They walked back to the house in silence. Jem sensed that Mirabelle didn't want to talk. She cast occasional glances in her direction, but Mirabelle stared straight ahead, her eyes fixed on the road, jaw clenched, as if on a path toward some dreadful destiny from which she couldn't turn away. Sometimes Mirabelle murmured softly to Piglet, but Jem was afraid to look for fear Piglet might become a mountain of eyes or teeth, or something spiked and clawed that breathed fire.

Despite this fear she couldn't help asking the question that had been plaguing her since she'd first set eyes on Piglet.

"What *is* he?"

Jem held on tight to Tom. There was just the gentle sound of a breeze rustling through leaves in the dark before Mirabelle eventually answered.

"He's family," she said.

Tom coughed, and the small, dark creature stirred, and

despite what Mirabelle just said, Jem squeezed her eyes shut for a second and prayed that Piglet wouldn't wake up.

They walked in silence the rest of the way. It seemed that nothing but forest lay ahead, but then Mirabelle put her hand out for Jem, and with two more steps she felt a sensation of passing through something. Jem was dimly aware of a slight shimmering as they stepped through the Glamour and suddenly they were on the grounds of the estate. They walked through the main gate and up the driveway. The silence was suffocating, all-encompassing, and Jem felt the hairs on the back of her neck prickle as she saw the shadowy figures waiting on the steps up ahead.

Enoch stood there in his familiar pose, chin up, hands clasped behind his back. Odd, Eliza, Bertram, Dotty, and Daisy all stood alongside him.

"A serious crime has been committed," said Enoch, his voice ringing out in the night.

Jem didn't like his tone, and she liked the disdain in his eyes even less as he glanced at Tom.

"Yes, yes it has, Uncle," said Mirabelle flatly.

"Well then, something must be done about it," said Enoch, glaring at Jem. "A crime cannot go unpunished."

"No, a crime cannot go unpunished," agreed Mirabelle quietly.

Jem felt a fluttering sensation in her chest, and a growing sense of panic, as if the ground were sliding out from under her feet.

Enoch nodded. "Good, I see that you agree. Well then, with that in mind—"

"What punishment do you think you deserve, Uncle?" said Mirabelle, a little louder now.

Jem sensed a ripple of unease in the dark. The members of the Family seemed somehow smaller to her now. She couldn't help but think about the terrified cows they'd encountered earlier in the field.

Enoch gave a quick bark of laughter, but Mirabelle was not deterred. She kept looking at him, unblinking, as if waiting for something.

"What if I just woke Piglet up again? How would that suit as punishment?" Mirabelle said, looking pointedly at the small furry creature asleep in her arms.

Bertram was whimpering, and Jem was convinced the others had become even paler.

"He is very dangerous, as you've often said. And now I know why," said Mirabelle through clenched teeth, her eyes shadowed with weariness.

Enoch shook his head and sighed, but Jem could tell by the way his shoulders slumped that he knew he was beaten.

"Mirabelle, please . . ."

"Where did I come from?"

Enoch looked at the ground.

"Who was she? Who was that woman I saw?"

Enoch rubbed his forehead and refused to look at Mirabelle.

"I saw you at the window holding a baby. Why were you crying, Enoch?"

Enoch's eyes widened in shock.

He looked helpless, and Jem felt a sudden pity for him that took her by surprise. He seemed lost, like a man who has suddenly entered a strange new world and has no idea where he is. She knew how that felt.

"Mirabelle . . ."

"Enoch, just tell me. Who was she?"

Enoch sighed and closed his eyes.

Eliza stepped forward. "She was your mother."

Enoch looked furious with her, but Eliza simply ignored him and continued speaking to Mirabelle.

"She was your mother, and I'm sorry we hid that from you, and that you had to find out this way. We all thought it was for the best. We thought . . ." She shook her head.

It seemed as if the whole night exhaled. All eyes were on Mirabelle. She looked at a point in the middle distance, as if no one else was there. Eventually she nodded.

"Right, I see." She started up the steps. "I need to get Piglet back to his room."

The Family parted and watched her enter the house.

Jem took Tom up the steps, but he stopped her when they reached the top and shook his head. He pushed her away gently and made his way over to Enoch. A shocked Enoch could only stare as Tom gave his arm a squeeze.

"You shouldn't blame yourself. You did your best for her," said Tom.

He turned and stumbled slightly. Jem grabbed hold of him and walked him into the house. She took him upstairs, and his strength seemed to rally a little. He removed his bloody shirt before clambering into bed. Tom looked up at the ceiling. He seemed calm despite everything that had happened.

"You should find Mirabelle," he said.

"How do you feel?"

"I'm fine. I'll be fine," he said, smiling weakly. "Go and find Mirabelle."

Mirabelle was locking the great iron door to Piglet's room when Jem found her. For some reason she didn't feel afraid about venturing down into this part of the house anymore.

Mirabelle leaned her forehead against the door. "You were right, you know."

"About what?" asked Jem.

Mirabelle turned and looked at her. Her gray eyes were clouded over with pain. She laid a hand on her chest.

"It hurts. It hurts everywhere."

Freddie

The panicked hammering on the front door came in the early hours of the morning. Freddie jolted awake with his heart pounding. He'd been dreaming of James again. They'd been driving past some fields with their father, and James was smiling and laughing and telling him a story. Freddie was laughing so hard tears came to his eyes. He turned to see his father at the wheel. He was laughing also, and the green fields whizzed by, and the world was bright and filled with promise, and Freddie wanted it to last forever . . .

But then came that panicked knocking. Freddie hopped out of bed, immediately slathered in sweat. He opened his bedroom window, which was above the butcher's shop and faced right out onto the main street.

"Hello?" he said.

A short, but stocky figure stepped back from the door. It was Mr. Carswell, one of the local farmers.

"Freddie! Get your dad. Something's happened."

Freddie woke his father. It was like watching a great balding giant lumbering out of the bed in the dark. Freddie's mother stirred, and his father assured her that there was nothing to worry about.

Freddie let Mr. Carswell in while his father got dressed. Mr. Carswell had a bushy lion's mane of a beard while what was left of his gray hair stood out from the top of his head in corkscrews. Today his agitation had made his hair even more askew. He looked out the window, patting the knuckles of one hand fretfully against the palm of the other.

"What is it, Bill?"

Freddie's father loomed in the doorway, like a great hulking shadow hewn from the very night. Freddie hadn't even heard him approach. Mr. Carswell looked at him and licked his lips.

"Something terrible's happened, Frank."

Mr. Fletcher took the farmer aside for a moment. They had a whispered conversation out of earshot, but Freddie could tell by his father's whole demeanor that something very serious was going on. The only words he caught were "They wouldn't! We have an agreement!" from his father. Freddie's mind was suddenly a whirl as he considered what those words meant.

They drove to the farm in silence, following Mr. Carswell's car. Freddie's father planned for his son to take over his seat on the council one day. That meant Freddie needed to go with him whenever there was a crisis of "this sort." "For experience," his father had said. "This sort" usually meant something that was linked to the House of Rookhaven. After all, that was the council's main reason for existing, to deal with all matters pertaining to their agreement with the Family. It was a thought that made Freddie feel uneasy about what lay ahead.

As the road slipped by, he found himself thinking about that dream again, and how they'd been driving down a similar country road blessed with sunlight, and how James had been laughing and his father had been smiling . . .

"What are you smiling about?" his father said sharply. He'd asked the question without taking his eyes off the road.

Freddie shook his head. "Nothing, Dad." He turned and looked at the space on the seat between him and the van door. The space where James would have been sitting.

Freddie had seen plenty of dead cows before. But they'd been slabs of meat prepared for sale. He'd never seen anything like this.

A light drizzle was pattering on the leaves of the trees around them. Mr. Carswell was wringing his hands, and Freddie felt a flush of embarrassment when he realized that the poor man was crying.

"What happened ain't natural, Frank. It ain't."

Freddie's father squinted at the remains of the cow. "Dogs, maybe. A pack of them. That's what I'm thinking."

Mr. Carswell shook his head furiously, and even in the dark Freddie could see the red glow of fury on his face.

"Not dogs. Not ever. This was unnatural. Unnatural. We know who done this. It was them up in the house."

Freddie's father ran a hand over his head and sighed.

Mr. Carswell continued, his fury building. "Think of all we've done for them. Think of all we've gone without during the war because of them and that agreement that was made. And what do we get in return? Nothing! That's what. Just . . ." He gestured helplessly at the remains of the cow. "We need to call the council together, Frank. This won't stand. It can't stand."

As Freddie and his father drove back home, Freddie could feel the tension almost crackling in the air. He'd seen the panic and anger in his father's eyes at the sight of the dead cow. He could tell by the way his father was gripping the steering wheel that he was unnerved.

"Dogs." His father nodded to himself, then looked at Freddie. "Dogs. That's most likely it. A pack of dogs gone feral."

Freddie nodded, but he knew his father was only trying to convince himself. There was something more to this incident, but he didn't dare question his father about it. He didn't want to rock the boat by agreeing with Mr. Carswell. He felt too absurdly grateful for being included in what was an all-too-rare conversation with his father.

Freddie turned to look out the window, and their headlights illuminated something on the side of the road.

For a moment, Freddie felt an electric charge envelop his whole body.

"Dad?"

His father had seen the same thing. He put the car into reverse and moved slowly back along the road.

Freddie's heart started thumping. It was all right. He was with his father. Everything would be okay. Whatever it was they'd seen, his father could deal with it.

But it was only a man.

The man waved at them from the side of the road. He wore a wide-brimmed leather hat and a leather coat so large it looked almost like a tent. Freddie felt relief wash over him. He was certain he'd seen something else.

They pulled up alongside, and the man picked up a battered old carryall and stepped toward the passenger window. He looked to be in his fifties, with a lined face and a broad smile. Brown hair streaked with gray spilled out from beneath the brim of his hat.

Freddie rolled down the window on his father's instruction, and the man leaned in, his impossibly large smile broadening even more.

"Well, what a nice surprise on a night so filled with unpleasantness." He nodded down the road. "I was traveling myself. Alas, my own poor car gave up the ghost quite a way back." He looked contrite. "I don't suppose I could trouble you for a lift to the nearest town?"

"Hop in," said Mr. Fletcher.

The man climbed in beside Freddie and placed his carryall in the footwell. There was a constant clinking from it as if it contained lots of empty milk bottles.

He leaned across Freddie to shake Mr. Fletcher's hand, and Freddie instinctively leaned back to avoid touching him. The man's coat smelled musty and old. It had gray patches of what looked like mildew on it.

"Arnold Pheeps," said the man, shaking Mr. Fletcher's hand vigorously.

"Frank Fletcher, and this is my son Freddie."

Mr. Pheeps smiled at Freddie. "How pleasantly alliterative. I'm very pleased to meet you, Freddie."

The man's hand felt dry and papery. His grip was limp, and Freddie didn't like the way he looked at him with those wide dark-blue eyes.

Mr. Pheeps settled back in his seat and sighed with satisfaction.

"And where, pray tell, are we going?" asked Mr. Pheeps.

Freddie didn't like his tone. There was something slightly mocking in it, and Freddie felt as if his father were now being treated like the man's personal chauffeur. But it didn't seem to bother his father.

"The village of Rookhaven."

Mr. Pheeps nodded. "A village. How nice. And what a lovely name." He suddenly clenched his fists and thrust his head forward, his eyes wide with excitement. "Is there anything on this earth quite like a village? Is there anything to compare to the rigor and strength of its bonds of community and fellowship, particularly after a time of great darkness? I think not, Mr. Fletcher. I think not. What say you?"

Mr. Fletcher nodded. "I suppose not, Mr. Pheeps."

Mr. Pheeps pursed his lips and looked rather pleased with himself. "You are a kindred spirit, then."

The car rumbled along through the dark. Freddie tried to concentrate on its rhythms, hoping they might lull him into drowsiness the way they had when he was younger and they'd all be driving home at night after a family outing, but it was difficult. He could sense Mr. Pheeps looking at him.

"And you, young Freddie? Do you have any siblings?"

Freddie felt his chest tighten. He looked at his hands.

"No, sir, my brother . . ."

There was a pause. Mr. Fletcher cleared his throat.

"I had an older son, Mr. Pheeps. He fought in the war."

Had. Freddie suddenly hated that word so much.

"My condolences to you and your family," said Mr. Pheeps, closing his eyes in sympathy. "Although it must be some small consolation to you that he fought for noble ideals against a great evil and won."

"It is," said Mr. Fletcher, his voice tight and small in the narrow confines of the cab.

"You'll need somewhere to stay until your car's fixed," said Mr. Fletcher, trying to brighten his tone. "You're welcome to lodge with us. We have an extra room."

Freddie felt his stomach plummet.

"I wouldn't want to impose, Mr. Fletcher. Surely you have enough on your plate."

"It's no trouble at all, Mr. Pheeps. What kind of people would we be if we didn't welcome strangers? It's no trouble."

"Well, I am humbled by your offer, and I accept." He wagged his finger. "But I don't intend on becoming an encumbrance, even for a short stay."

Mr. Pheeps chuckled, and Freddie was surprised to see his father almost smile.

They arrived at the village, and Mr. Pheeps oohed and aahed at how "singular and charming" it all was. Freddie could sense the man looking at him again, as if trying to draw him into conversation, but Freddie ignored him and kept his eyes fixed firmly in front.

They parked outside their shop, and Mr. Pheeps apologized for the clinking his bag made. He spotted Freddie looking at the bag and he patted it.

"Various medicinals and concoctions which keep me sustained. I am no longer in my prime, after all."

That big broad smile again. A smile with too many teeth. Freddie found it difficult to look at.

His father opened the door at the side of the shop that led into the house. He motioned for Mr. Pheeps to enter, but the man paused for a moment to take in a deep lungful of air. The rain had stopped, and the air was clear and sweet.

"How lovely," he said, then stepped over the threshold, followed by Mr. Fletcher.

That was when Freddie felt sickest of all. The man was strange, and Freddie didn't like his smile or his attitude. He didn't entirely trust the man. But what bothered Freddie most was what he'd seen at first back on the road.

Because what he'd seen wasn't a man.

Freddie was convinced it had been something else. Something skeletal with flesh barely clinging to its bones. Something with a long face and a dark gash of a mouth stretched perpetually down in what looked like a silent howl. That howling mouth was packed with impossibly long, yellowed teeth. Then there were the eyes. Two slimy, gray, meaty marbles that flicked back and forth agitatedly.

Eyes that seemed to be searching for something.

Piglet

Piglet feels guilty here in the dark.

He didn't mean to do any harm. He only wanted to play. Now he can sense the confusion in the house, a babble of thoughts and voices that has a keen edge to it, and something running through it all that he has never understood before, but feels he understands now ...

Piglet doesn't want to think about it. He shakes his head and makes himself as small as possible in a quiet corner in the dark. Makes himself so small that surely no one will see him ever again.

Or find him.

And that's the most important thing of all. Piglet does not want to be found. Something new has stirred inside him since his adventure, something he has never previously felt.

He can sense the change in the house and even further away. The sense of something shifting, like an ancient stone moved from its foundation and now rolling inexorably downhill.

Piglet sees things. In the Room of Knives the ravens sit silently among the rafters between the shafts of moonlight, their watchful eyes glittering in the dark. Somewhere a boy stands with his father at the door of their home. A man who is not a man pauses at the threshold of the same door and sniffs the night air and smiles.

To Piglet that smile is as sharp as a scythe.

And for the first time in his life Piglet is afraid.

Part 3
Comes the Malice

Mirabelle

The images that came to Mirabelle after that fateful night were like blackened and burnt wisps of paper floating on a breeze. Piglet had somehow pieced together a near-complete history of the house and its inhabitants, even from the depths of his room. Mirabelle sensed this in the images that had been seared into her mind through their encounter—the comings and goings of the Family down through the generations. Piglet hadn't revealed everything, but he'd revealed enough.

When she was least expecting it, an image would appear. There was no rhyme or reason to their order. She had a vision of Enoch looking up at the house for the first time, the blinding white light of the moon illuminating his face.

She saw Bertram eating triangular sandwiches in the dining room, holding them delicately between thumb and forefinger, his pinkie finger extended, while Aunt Eliza sat at the other end of the table reading from a book, pausing occasionally to sigh and roll her eyes.

Odd appearing from a portal wearing oilskins. Water sloshing around the edges of the portal while he swiped with a steel pike at the tentacles of some great sea beast that sought to squeeze through the opening before it closed.

Shadows arriving up the path leading to the house. Men

from the village. Enoch waiting for them at the entrance to the estate, Odd and Eliza with him. And somehow Mirabelle knew this was all a long time ago.

Enoch flying through the night sky, looking for a flower that had uprooted itself and was now wandering the estate.

Dr. Ellenby making his way down the Path of Flowers back toward the village while rain poured down and lightning crashed around him. He was hunched forward, his hands deep in his coat pockets, while the flowers watched him, forbidden to touch such a senior member of the council.

Odd appearing from a portal in the garden in brilliant sunshine, wearing a police constable's helmet and carrying a bunch of exotic flowers.

Then at night in the rain, his hair plastered to his head, watching a car make its way up the driveway.

Odd sitting on the roof of the house and looking at the stars as the last remnants of the rainclouds drifted away. His hair still damp. His eyes glittering with tears.

And the woman.

Sometimes she was walking through the garden, usually alone. Once she was with Uncle Enoch, talking outside the house. Enoch was smiling and he looked younger somehow.

Whenever she saw these images of the woman (*her mother, how could she be her mother?*), Mirabelle felt a wrenching in her heart, as if she were hollowed out somehow, empty. It was something she had never experienced before. It burned. And yes. She felt that feeling everywhere.

She tried several times to talk to Enoch and get him to answer questions about what she'd seen, but he'd barricaded himself in his study. He seemed more concerned with the possible problem the incident with Piglet might cause with the village. This only angered Mirabelle even more.

Today she watched from a second-floor window as Mr. Fletcher's van arrived in the driveway, even though it wasn't delivery day. Two cars followed. One was Dr. Ellenby's battered old Ford. Enoch and Aunt Eliza were the official receiving party at the front door.

Freddie's father stepped out of his van as the others pulled up alongside. Mirabelle stared at the members of the council below and, for some reason, felt nothing but hatred for them. It wasn't their fault, she supposed. She reserved most of her anger for the Family, who lied to her, but she had a slight suspicion that these men had somehow also been involved.

Mr. Fletcher was wearing a gray pinstriped suit. It was slightly too tight on him, and he looked uncomfortable, shifting his weight awkwardly from foot to foot as he waited for his companions to join him. It wouldn't do for him to greet Enoch alone, Mirabelle supposed, what with the council being so obsessed with formality and their stupid old customs. She sneered inwardly and felt guilty at the same time, a burning feeling she couldn't understand.

Mr. Teasdale, the local postmaster, stepped out of one car. He was a short, nervous-looking man dressed in tweed, with a high pink color to his face and round spectacles. He looked around him, his hands in his pockets in an obvious effort to appear relaxed. In Mirabelle's opinion, it only made him look more awkward.

Reverend Dankworth, a long, tall wisp of man, climbed out of the passenger seat with the slow, long-legged grace of a spider emerging from a crack in a skirting board. Dr. Ellenby was the last to join the group.

They made their way stiffly to Enoch and Eliza, shaking hands and nodding somberly. There was a pause while they all stood and looked at each other, then Enoch waved them into the house. Dr. Ellenby looked up as he went in, caught sight of Mirabelle, and waved.

Mirabelle didn't respond and simply stepped back from the window.

"Is something happening?"

Mirabelle hadn't heard Jem approaching. She was standing a few steps away, picking at the cuff of her cardigan.

"It's a council meeting," said Mirabelle, "*the first of its kind in many generations*," she added, mimicking the self-important tone that Enoch had used as he'd announced it to the senior members of the Family this morning when he'd thought Mirabelle wasn't listening.

But Mirabelle *had* been listening, listening to everything: to the whispers she heard before she rounded a corner and caught Bertram conversing guiltily with Odd, to the murmuring of Eliza and Enoch behind his closed study door.

And then there was Piglet.

Piglet had been completely silent since that night. He hadn't made a sound. Mirabelle wondered why. She'd gone to visit him, but tapping his door had yielded no response. She'd never known Piglet to be so quiet. She found it unsettling.

"What will they be talking about?" asked Jem.

"Isn't it obvious?" said Mirabelle, a little too sharply. "Sorry," she said, seeing the look of surprise on Jem's face.

"It's all right," said Jem. "Things have been ..."

"Strange," said Mirabelle, allowing herself a wry smile.

"That's putting it mildly," said Jem.

"How's Tom?"

"Still resting. He seems different somehow." Jem looked slightly uncomfortable for a moment. "I never thanked you."

Mirabelle frowned. "For what?"

"For saving me from ... from ... from whatever ..." Jem gestured uselessly, as if words weren't enough.

"Piglet meant no harm," said Mirabelle, suddenly feeling very protective of him.

Jem nodded.

"He's just curious, I think," said Mirabelle.

"Tom says he knows things. That Piglet can see into people's minds."

"He can," said Mirabelle. "But I don't think he fully understands them."

"Well, that makes two of us," said Jem, chuckling slightly.

"Enoch won't talk to me."

"Maybe he's afraid to," said Jem.

"Afraid?"

"He seemed very shaken when you confronted him after Piglet's escape," said Jem.

Mirabelle snorted. "You mean he's afraid of me?"

"No, not of you exactly. I think he thought he was doing his best for you."

"By lying to me?"

Jem looked pensive. "And what happened after Piglet escaped might have brought back painful memories for him."

Mirabelle considered this. The Enoch she'd seen when Piglet's mind touched hers had seemed different, wounded somehow. But did that excuse his keeping things from her? She didn't think so.

Mirabelle had a sudden thought. "Would you like to do something?"

"Like what?" asked Jem.

Mirabelle grinned. "Cause trouble."

Mirabelle experienced a delicious little stab of pleasure when she saw the looks on the faces of the council as she burst into the dining room. Mr. Teasdale blinked in panic, looking from one council member to another, as if asking them to confirm what he was seeing. A muscle in Reverend

Dankworth's right cheek twitched, and he looked both uneasy and slightly disgusted. Mr. Fletcher's demeanor didn't change. His fists were balled on the table in front of him, and he was his usual barely restrained, furious self.

Uncle Enoch clasped his hands together, knocked his thumbs against his forehead, and sighed heavily.

"What is it, Mirabelle?"

Mirabelle shrugged. "I'm not sure, Uncle. Is it a birthday party? Where's the cake?"

Mirabelle noticed Odd trying to mask a chuckle.

There was a screech of wood on the floor as Mr. Teasdale jumped up from his chair and pointed at her.

"She shouldn't be here!" he shrieked.

Mirabelle shrugged. "Who's to say who should or shouldn't be anywhere?"

Now it was Aunt Eliza's turn to suppress a smile.

"Nor should she," said Reverend Dankworth, nodding at

Jem, who was standing behind Mirabelle.

"She's my guest," said Mirabelle, "and this is my home. I'm permitted to take guests anywhere I want in my own home."

"She's an outsider," said Dankworth, "and as such she is not party to the Covenant and must leave."

Mirabelle looked at Jem, then at Reverend Dankworth.

"*She* isn't leaving."

Murmurs rippled around the room as the men conversed with each other. Mirabelle was conscious of the many furtive glances being thrown in her direction, but only one of the villagers was looking her directly in the eye.

"Dr. Ellenby, can you explain to me what exactly seems to be the problem?" said Mirabelle.

Dr. Ellenby, to his credit, kept his eyes locked with hers, and he seemed to be about to say something when Enoch laid a hand on his arm.

"Marcus is bound by council rules, and as such he cannot—"

"What am I, Uncle?"

Mirabelle noticed the swift flush on Dr. Ellenby's cheeks, the way Enoch's eyes widened ever so slightly, and the way the rest of the men around the table froze.

"It's a simple question, Uncle. What am I?"

"Mirabelle . . ." Enoch looked pained.

"Where did I come from? I didn't come from the Ether, did I?"

"Mirabelle, please . . ."

Freddie

Freddie's mother was stirring a pot on the stove when her husband came in the door. She exchanged a knowing glance with Freddie.

"Ludicrous," Freddie's father growled as he sat down at the dining table.

"What's ludicrous, dear?" said Freddie's mother, her tone light.

"We had a meeting about the incident, and it was disrupted by that girl."

"Mirabelle," said Freddie, instinctively annoyed that his father wouldn't use her name.

"Have you done those accounts yet?" his father snapped.

Freddie shook his head. His father shifted uncomfortably in his chair, his face twitching when he caught his wife's warning glance.

"Just try and get them done before the end of the day," he said, his voice a little gentler.

Freddie nodded. His father had him do the accounts because he reckoned it would help him "become a responsible individual," as he described it. Freddie knew he was being groomed to take over the shop some day.

"They say they'll do penance for what happened with the incident and that thing getting out. If you ask me, it isn't enough."

"What was her name?" Mirabelle shouted. She was trembling with a rage so strong that it almost brought her to tears.

Dr. Ellenby lowered his eyes and looked at the table.

Mirabelle took a moment to compose herself. She was conscious that Jem was by her shoulder, and the very fact that she was nearby lent Mirabelle some measure of calm. She looked at them all and closed a fist round her pendant.

"I don't know what I am."

She looked each of them in the eye in turn.

"But maybe there's one way of finding out."

Mirabelle took the pendant from her neck and flung it onto the table. Some of the men flinched. The pendant skimmed across the surface and came to rest with a rattle in front of Enoch.

"I'm going outside," she said.

She turned her back on them and headed toward the door. She experienced a grim satisfaction when she felt the movement of air behind her, as if they'd all risen at once. Enoch's shout of "Mirabelle!" was the icing on the cake.

Jem was instantly by her side. "Mirabelle."

Mirabelle squeezed her shoulder. "I know what I'm doing."

The truth was she had no idea what she was doing, but she felt compelled by some greater force, by rage, by grief. She had to know.

Enoch shouted again as she made her way across the

hallway toward the front door. Mirabelle heard the unfurling of wings, and the nervous gibbering of Mr. Teasdale and Reverend Dankworth behind her. Enoch rushed overhead and landed in front of the door, his wings spread wide, his face still human in aspect.

"You can't," he said, and Mirabelle was surprised by the pleading in his voice.

Mirabelle stopped before him and looked up at him defiantly.

"I can, Uncle. And I will."

They stared at each other for a few moments, then Enoch looked away and Mirabelle knew she had won. She walked past him and stepped out, into the cool shadows that shaded the steps, hesitating just for a moment. She looked at Jem.

"What's it like, walking in sunlight unprotected?" she asked.

Jem shook her head. She was at a loss as to how to explain it.

Mirabelle stood on the last step. She closed her eyes.

Then she jumped.

She was aware of a strange sensation. Without her pendant she was exposed to the light of the sun. For the first time in her life she felt its rays. She stretched out her arms and laughed.

She opened her eyes and looked at the crowd of people collected at the front door. She winked at Enoch.

"Look, Uncle. Look at me. I didn't burn."

She looked at the dark patch on the ground.

"Sorry, Great-Uncle Cornelius, I don't mean to mock."

She looked at Jem.

"What do you call this, this feeling?" she asked Jem, rubbing her hands together as she felt a strange sensation that seemed to coat her skin.

"You're feeling warm," said Jem.

"Warm," said Mirabelle in wonder. She turned to those gathered at the door. "Go, have your meeting. I'm going to play in the sun with my friend."

Freddie's mother took some bowls over to the table and laid them out.

"A cow got disemboweled and eaten, dear. There's no need to be coy—you are a butcher after all. *Incident* indeed."

Freddie's father was rocking agitatedly in his chair. He looked at Freddie with a gaze that almost made him flinch. It contained hurt, fear, and anger. Freddie hadn't seen his father so agitated since . . .

He couldn't think about that. He couldn't think about James. He scribbled down some more figures and tried to block the world out.

"Oh dear, it sounds like you do have a lot on your mind, Mr. Fletcher."

Mr. Pheeps was leaning nonchalantly against the doorjamb with his arms folded. He was still wearing that awful coat of his. With his straggly hair and wide mouth, Freddie found it strangely difficult to look at him for too long.

"That we do, Mr. Pheeps," said Freddie's father.

He said it in the pompous, self-important tone that both Freddie and his mother recognized as his "I am about council business" tone. It implied that he was doing the most important work in the world. Freddie's mother ladled vegetable soup into bowls, and she took a moment to look at Freddie and rolled her eyes.

"And tell me, what difficulties are you currently dealing with?" asked Mr. Pheeps.

"If you must know, Mr. Pheeps, we are currently having troubles with the inhabitants of the local estate."

Freddie didn't like the way his father sat up higher in his chair when Mr. Pheeps spoke. He'd noticed that since they'd first met him, his father always seemed very eager to please him. Almost as if the man had some kind of hold over him.

Mr. Pheeps tilted his head and rubbed his hands together. "Estate? Which estate might that be? I've seen no *estate* in these parts."

"That's because it's been hidden," said Mr. Fletcher.

Mr. Pheeps's mouth was an O of wonder, his eyes flicking back and forth, as if calculating something. Freddie felt a sudden wave of panic. He wanted to scream for his father to stop talking.

"Hidden, you say? Hidden how?"

Mr. Pheeps tilted his head again. Freddie's scalp felt as if things were crawling on it.

Mr. Fletcher looked slightly abashed. "Well, I'm not sure I can say—"

"You can't say," said Freddie's mother, banging some spoons down on the table. "Would you like some soup, Mr. Pheeps? You're welcome to join us," she said without looking at him.

Mr. Pheeps gave his best supercilious smile. "I think I shall politely decline the offer, Mrs. Fletcher, as generous as it is."

Mrs. Fletcher nodded while keeping her eyes on her soup.

"Why don't you join us for dinner this evening, then?" suggested Mr. Fletcher.

Mr. Pheeps beamed with delight. Freddie's heart felt like a lead weight that was sinking straight to the floor.

"How very kind of you. I think I shall accept the invitation. It may give us some time to talk through your troubles, Mr. Fletcher. They seem to weigh so heavily upon you, and you have been so hospitable to me that I feel it would be remiss of me not to pay you due attention and perhaps provide some advice."

Freddie could see his mother's jaw hardening. He could feel Mr. Pheeps's eyes on the family, and he fought the urge to look at him because to look at him would mean seeing that nauseating smile again.

"I shall leave you in peace," Mr. Pheeps said, withdrawing.

A few moments passed. The only sound in the kitchen was the gentle slurping of soup. Freddie's mother eventually broke the silence.

"I really don't like that man."

After his soup, Freddie went for one of his customary walks. People on the street nodded and greeted him as he passed. Freddie liked that about Rookhaven: everyone knew everyone else, and there was always a sense that they were looking out for one another, especially since the war. Especially since . . .

Freddie stopped himself. It was best not to think about those things. It was best to move on, that's what he overheard his father say to his mum once when they thought he hadn't been listening.

He passed Mr. Biggins the tailor, a craggy-faced man in a gray suit. He was always whistling a tune. He was whistling one now as he walked down the street and tipped his hat to Freddie. Freddie recognized the song as "We'll Gather Lilacs." It was a song his mum liked, and she always paused in whatever she was doing when it came on the wireless. Freddie grinned and saluted him back. Mr. Biggins kept whistling and winked at him.

On the other side of the road, Mrs. Smith was helping her husband take in the fruit from outside their greengrocery. She saw Freddie and waved him over.

"All right, Freddie? How are you?" she asked.

"Good, thanks, Mrs. Smith," said Freddie.

"And your mum and dad?"

"Good," said Freddie.

"Take this," said Mrs. Smith, offering him an apple.

Freddie started patting his pockets. "But I don't have my ration book."

Mr. Smith snorted as he carried a tray of vegetables back into the shop. "Ration book."

"Here," said Mrs. Smith, forcing the apple into Freddie's hand.

Freddie pocketed it, not knowing what to say. Both he and Mrs. Smith turned when they heard the familiar tap on the footpath.

Alfie Parkin was making his way toward them.

"Hello," Alfie said, his voice quiet as he made his way past. He gave a wan smile.

"Hello, Alfie. Lovely afternoon."

They watched him make his way down the street.

"That poor boy," said Mrs. Smith quietly.

Mr. Smith stood in the doorway, his hand on the doorjamb. "At least he made it home," he said. Mrs. Smith's lip trembled, and Freddie remembered her sons Arthur and David, and turned away to save her embarrassment.

To Freddie it sometimes felt as if a great pall lay over the village.

As soon as he crossed the boundary between the village and the trees, Freddie began to feel airy and light again. He always felt freer here. The sun was shining, and the sound of the breeze in the trees was restful. That great pall lifted. He could forget his father's simmering rage, the dark, haunted hollows of his eyes, the way his mother would occasionally stop during the washing up and just look vacantly out of the window.

Freddie heard someone talking to his right. He followed the sound of the voice.

He rounded a tree and smiled when he saw Kevin Bennett kneeling on the ground. There was no mistaking his unruly shock of blond hair.

"All right, Kev? What have you got there?"

Kevin turned round, his eyes big behind his thick-rimmed glasses.

"It's a bird," he said.

A tiny wagtail was wheeling around in circles on the ground, dragging a broken wing. Freddie approached slowly, not wanting to panic it any further.

"What should we do?" asked Kevin.

Freddie knelt beside Kevin and gently picked up the bird. He could feel the panicked thrumming of its tiny heart, and for one second he was terrified it might burst, so he moved as slowly as he could, shushing the bird, stroking its feathers as gently as possible.

"It needs a splint," he said.

Kevin pushed his glasses up his nose and squinted hard at the bird.

"Will it die?" he whispered, as if afraid to say the words out loud.

Freddie smiled at him. He took in Kevin's moth-eaten tank top and his battered black shoes, which were one size too big for him.

"It won't die," he said.

"Can I?" said Kevin, reaching out a hand to pet the bird.

"Course you can."

Kevin stroked the bird gently, while it cheeped and fluttered between Freddie's palms.

"We'll look after you, little birdy," said Kevin, his voice filled with awe.

Freddie felt a sudden warmth, a rightness. They would

take the bird to his house and nurse it back to health. Everything would be . . .

"Hello, boys, what have you got there?"

Freddie froze with the bird cupped in his hands. He didn't want to turn around. He wished that the bird's wing could magically heal itself right now and that it could fly far, far away from this place, become a speck in the sky.

"Let me see," said the voice.

Freddie turned to find Mr. Pheeps standing a few feet away from them, his head tilted in curiosity.

"It's nothing," said Freddie.

"Nothing?" said Mr. Pheeps, his lip curling.

"It's just a bird," Kevin blurted.

Freddie could hear Kevin's breath coming in short, panicked gasps. Mr. Pheeps leaned forward with his hands on his knees.

"And who do we have here? What's your name, young man?"

He smiled that impossibly wide smile. Kevin shook his head frantically.

"His face," Kevin whispered to Freddie, "what's wrong with his face?"

"Run," Freddie hissed at him.

Kevin didn't need to be told twice. He pelted away, while Freddie positioned himself between Mr. Pheeps and the fleeing boy.

Mr. Pheeps advanced toward Freddie with the slow, steady steps of a predator. Freddie wanted to run too, but he fought the urge. He wanted to show this man . . .

This thing, this thing.

. . . that he wasn't afraid of him.

Mr. Pheeps waved him forward. "Let me see."

Freddie moved toward the man . . .

This thing.

. . . because he would not give him the pleasure of showing any fear. But his legs were shaking.

Mr. Pheeps cupped his own hands, and Freddie laid the bird in them, immediately feeling like a traitor as it chirruped.

Mr. Pheeps looked at it with feigned concern.

"Blessed little thing."

He stroked its feathers gently with his index finger.

"Tell me, Freddie. Were you proud of him?"

Freddie's voice felt tight and strangled.

"What?"

Mr. Pheeps shook his head patronizingly. "Oh, Freddie. Your brother, of course. Were you proud of him?"

Freddie swallowed. "Yes, I was . . . I am proud of him."

Now Mr. Pheeps gave him a look of mocking pity. "I was? I am?"

Freddie felt tears spring to his eyes.

Mr. Pheeps turned his attention back to the bird. The bird was trembling.

Mr. Pheeps sighed. "Is it true that he never came home?"

Freddie swallowed hard. The world was starting to blur. He nodded.

"But you, in your quietest moments, you imagine that he's simply lost, don't you?"

Freddie looked at the ground.

"You imagine that he was merely injured and that he's forgotten who he is, and that some day he'll remember, and on that day he'll come home. That's what you imagine." Mr. Pheeps leaned over him. "That's what you hope." Pheeps made a mocking popping sound with his lips on the word "hope."

Freddie ran a sleeve across his eyes.

"I just think that's the saddest thing I've ever heard." He pouted at the bird. "Don't you think that's the saddest thing you've ever heard?"

"Stop it," said Freddie hoarsely.

"Stop what? Would you rather we discussed the truth? Would you rather I told you what I saw when I wandered through the world during the war? Would you rather I told you about the blood, the broken bones, the screams, the young men crying for their mothers? Would you rather I told you about one young man I saw in the dirt, looking up at me, his eyes pleading as the life drained from him? He could well have been your own brother."

Freddie was sobbing now.

"I see this is upsetting you. I'm so sorry, Freddie. Maybe

we could discuss something else. Why don't you tell me about the estate and the *people* who dwell within it?"

Freddie wiped his eyes. "No." He tried to take in a deep breath.

"No?"

"No," Freddie growled, angry now, despite his grief. "I've looked at your face. I've really looked at it, and I know one thing."

Mr. Pheeps looked genuinely surprised.

"I know it's not your real face," Freddie hissed through gritted teeth.

They both stared at each other for what seemed like a long time. Then Mr. Pheeps raised his cupped hands to his mouth. The bird was still trembling.

"Poor bird," he said. He puckered his lips and blew the faintest puff of air on it.

The bird stiffened briefly then went limp, its eyes glazing over. Mr. Pheeps opened his palms like a magician giving a final flourish, and the dead bird hit the ground with a soft *flump*.

Mr. Pheeps wiped his hands.

"I'll see you at dinner. Perhaps your good father will be more forthcoming."

Mr. Pheeps turned on his heel and left.

Freddie went down on his knees and looked at the bird. He wrapped his arms around himself, fighting his tears.

Jem

Jem and Mirabelle spent most of the afternoon on the grounds. Though they talked and laughed as normal, Jem couldn't help notice that Mirabelle seemed different in some way. Perhaps it was just that she was walking in sunlight. Perhaps it was something more.

They played a long game of hide-and-seek, during which Mirabelle had been like a thing possessed. She was breathless with excitement, and yet Jem could see something else in her eyes—a strange kind of rage.

After playing, they sat together in a small copse of trees and a long silence descended. Mirabelle played with a small pebble between her fingers and seemed to be pondering something.

"I don't know what I am," she said at last. "I'm not who I thought I was. I don't burn in sunlight, and now I know why I can't do anything. It's probably because I'm more human than the rest of the Family."

Jem desperately tried to think of something comforting to say.

"You don't need to eat or sleep," she blurted.

Mirabelle looked pained. "Well, that's very exciting, isn't it?"

She flung the pebble into the undergrowth.

Jem winced. "Are you thinking about her?" she asked.

Mirabelle nodded. "Sounds strange, doesn't it? I didn't know I had a mother, and suddenly because of Piglet I feel like I knew her, and now it feels like I've lost her."

She clasped her hands round her knees and breathed in viciously through her nose, rocking back and forth.

"It's like having hooks in my chest, and they tear."

Jem placed a hand on Mirabelle's shoulder. A sudden flapping sound distracted her. Four ravens landed on a branch above their heads, followed by the one-eyed raven from the house, who twitched his head and cawed imperiously to his companions. The others responded with their own throaty calls, and then the lead raven turned its one good eye to Jem and glared at her. It felt as if its gaze was burning right into her very soul.

"What are they doing?" she asked Mirabelle.

"Being nosy," said Mirabelle, standing up. She waved her arms at them. "Shoo, shoo," she shouted, but the ravens paid her no heed, and Jem could have sworn that the one-eyed raven cocked its beak snootily and turned its face away.

"*Cwaw cwaw*," it said, still turned away as if to express its indifference.

Mirabelle looked even more miserable. She shrugged at Jem.

"I still don't know what I am."

"You're my friend. For what it's worth."

Mirabelle managed a smile. The smile vanished as she

spotted something behind Jem, and Jem immediately felt her skin crawl.

One of the twins was standing right behind her. She was semivisible, and she was fiddling with her pendant and looking sorrowfully at the ground. Even Jem could guess who it was.

"What is it, Dotty?" Mirabelle asked.

Dotty looked up, tears in her translucent eyes. Jem found the effect very perturbing.

"I'm sorry, Mirabelle. It was all my fault."

"What was your fault?" asked Mirabelle.

Dotty clamped her lips tightly together and shook her head.

"Dotty?" Mirabelle looked at her.

"They think it was the boy."

"What?" asked Jem.

"Enoch and the others, they think it was the boy's fault, that he stole the key, because he's a thief." Dotty looked hurriedly at Jem. "No offense."

Jem felt a hot little twinge of anger at the comment.

"But it was me who gave it to him. I gave him the key to unlock Piglet's door."

There was silence in the copse, except for the sound of one raven ruffling its feathers. Mirabelle looked as shocked as Jem felt.

"Why? Why did you do that?" Mirabelle asked.

"Because I thought it would be fun."

Jem thought Mirabelle was about to launch herself at Dotty, and to be fair, she wouldn't have blamed her, but her friend just closed her eyes, took a moment to compose herself, and finally sighed.

"I see."

"In the end, though, it wasn't fun, was it?"

Mirabelle shook her head wearily. "No, Dotty, it wasn't."

"Are you angry with me?"

Mirabelle shook her head again.

"Are *you* cross with me?" asked Dotty, looking at Jem.

Jem was a little taken aback by the question, but she could only answer honestly.

"Yes. Yes, I am."

Dotty bit her lower lip and looked frightened. "You're not going to put me in a mirror like you did to Daisy, are you, Mirabelle?"

"No," said Mirabelle.

Dotty exhaled with relief. "Oh, good."

"But I will tell Enoch what you did unless you answer some questions for me."

Dotty looked crestfallen. Her eyes started to brim with more tears. Jem almost felt sorry for her.

"Who was my mother?"

"I don't know . . . I don't . . . I'm not allowed to even speak about it," she wailed.

There was a panicked movement above, and Jem looked up to see the ravens flapping agitatedly.

Mirabelle looked sternly at Dotty. "Why, Dotty?"

Dotty shook her head. "I don't know anything. Honest, I don't. Only *they* know, and they're the ones who decided to keep it secret."

"Who's they, Dotty?"

Dotty shook her head and clamped her mouth shut again.

"Enoch," said Mirabelle.

Dotty looked shamefaced.

"And who else?"

Dotty trembled. She was becoming solid now, as if she couldn't concentrate on staying transparent.

"Eliza? Uncle Bertram? Odd?"

The ravens continued to flap, as if urging her on.
Dotty shook her head.

Jem suddenly understood.

"No one else in the house knows, do they?" she said.

Dotty looked shocked.

Realization flashed across Mirabelle's face. "Dr. Ellenby!" she shouted.

The ravens began a chorus of caws. Dotty couldn't help but nod. Mirabelle glared up at the ravens.

"Just go away!"

The ravens took flight, wheeling for a moment above the trees before banking and heading for the house.

The silence was almost blessed now. Jem felt herself relax a little, despite the obvious manic light in Mirabelle's eyes as she spoke.

"Dr. Ellenby would know. He's the one person outside the house who Enoch really trusts. And he was there when . . ."

Mirabelle closed her eyes and swallowed, then she looked at Dotty.

"Go back to the house, Dotty. Don't tell anyone you were talking to me."

"I'd tell you anything if I could, Mirabelle, really I would—"

"Go back now, and talk to no one about this."

Dotty turned and walked away, taking a second to look back furtively at Mirabelle.

Jem could see the determination in Mirabelle's gray eyes.

"I'm going to talk to Dr. Ellenby," she said.

"When?"

"Tonight."

Jem felt the back of her neck tingle. She was speaking the words before she knew it.

"Then I'm coming with you."

Freddie

Dinner was a muted affair in the Fletcher household that evening.

Night was falling a lot quicker than expected. Freddie thought it was eerie, and while he knew it was irrational, he blamed the presence of Mr. Pheeps. The man sat to his left and gobbled down his steak-and-kidney pie, occasionally grinning at Freddie with a mouth full of meat and carrot and pastry. Freddie's parents were sitting to his right, but they seemed a whole world away.

"A most marvelous repast, Mrs. Fletcher," said Mr. Pheeps with his mouth full.

Freddie's mother nodded curtly. "Thank you, Mr. Pheeps."

"How lucky both these gentlemen are to have such a fine cook as you to look after them."

Freddie saw his mother bristle at that, but she kept her mouth shut. His father ate, as he so often did, mechanically, without saying a word, staring into space.

"I do, however, feel slightly guilty, what with rationing going on. You really are putting yourselves out to feed me. I feel . . . I feel as if I am taking something from you without giving anything in return."

"Not at all, Mr. Pheeps," said Mr. Fletcher.

Freddie tried to concentrate on his dinner, but all he could see was the bird, the forest air riffling through its feathers, its eyes blank.

Mr. Pheeps gave a small belch. He held a hand delicately to his stomach.

"Ooh, do excuse me." He patted his mouth with a fist. "In some countries such a thing would be considered a compliment."

Mr. Fletcher grunted.

Mr. Pheeps looked apologetic. "I have really enjoyed the dinner and company, but I do feel I must retire for the night. These old bones aren't what they used to be."

Mr. Pheeps bowed and scraped and left the room. The only noise now was the sound of cutlery on china plates. Freddie looked at his mother.

"May I be excused, Mum? I don't feel well."

"Boy should eat his dinner," his father grunted, still staring straight ahead.

Freddie's mum looked at him and nodded.

Freddie left the table, fully expecting his father to reprimand him, but he made it out into the hallway without him saying anything. Instead Freddie heard him use the word "penance" while talking to his mother. Something in the way he said it made Freddie stop in his tracks. He stood in the hall and listened.

"It's been decided," his father said.

"Who by?" his mother asked.

"There was a mutual agreement between both parties. It's

written into the Covenant. Any breaking of the rules results in penance."

"And what form will that penance take, Frank?"

Freddie could tell by the tone in his mother's voice that she didn't approve.

"They get no meat for a month."

"*They?*"

The tone of disgust in his mother's voice warmed Freddie's heart.

"Yes," his father replied. "They—"

"Use their names, Frank. Enoch and the others. They have names."

His father muttered something indecipherable, then raised his voice a little.

"They broke the Covenant. They're willing to pay the price. We have to restore trust. That thing got out and—"

"How do you know it's a thing?"

His father's response was garbled, and Freddie didn't hear anything from his mother, but he knew she would have her arms folded and be rolling her eyes.

"Then there's all that we've done for them, even during the war. We went without while they fattened their bellies on meat that should have been for our table. It's like what Mr. Pheeps said."

"And what's that?" asked Freddie's mother, a sliver of anger in her voice.

"They take and give nothing in return, and there's others

in the town too who think the same way. It's been going on long enough. It's time someone stood up and was counted and made our position clear."

Freddie didn't like what was being said. He'd never heard his father say a bad word about the Family before, and he reckoned his mother was just as shocked as he considered her silence.

He heard her muttering something, followed by the bang and slap of dishes and cutlery as she started the washing up.

Freddie crept away, preoccupied with what his father had said.

No lights were on at the rear of the house, and even though it was his home Freddie felt his skin tingling.

He heard something in the backyard, a distant sloshing sound. He went quietly through the scullery and opened the back door as slowly and carefully as possible.

The stillness of the night was broken by low guttural moans.

Freddie stepped into the backyard. The dry stink of old meat lent a tang to the air, and there was another smell too. He turned to his right to see Mr. Pheeps leaning almost drunkenly against a corner of the house. The cobbles at his feet were shiny and slick with vomit. Mr. Pheeps moaned.

"Are you all right?"

Freddie cursed himself for asking the question. It had been an instinctive response. Mr. Pheeps turned round, his arms limp, flapping in the air as if he'd lost the use of them.

He slid down the wall, sat on the ground, and threw his head back and laughed.

"Tell me, how do you stand that awful pig swill you call food?"

Freddie clenched his fists. Something had taken hold of him. He thought of the bird in the forest and what this thing had done to it, and for the moment he wasn't afraid.

"It's not pig swill. It's my mum's cooking."

Mr. Pheeps narrowed his eyes.

"Oh, we're suddenly very brave now, aren't we?"

Mr. Pheeps crossed his ankles and wiped a hand under his nose.

"You know, I don't get hungry very often, but when I do I like proper sustenance. I mean I can just about stomach some of what passes for your food to fit in, but really my dietary requirements are much more refined than . . ."

He waved his hand lazily at Freddie.

"To be honest, as long as I've walked this earth, I've never known what to call your kind."

Freddie took a step closer to Mr. Pheeps. Mr. Pheeps smiled, but his eyes were filled with contempt.

"What are you?" Freddie asked.

Mr. Pheeps shook his head and chuckled.

"Why are you here?"

Mr. Pheeps looked at him for a long time before answering. "I'm waiting," he said.

"For what?"

"The right moment. There's always a right moment, and that moment is almost here."

Mr. Pheeps stood up and dusted his coat off. He looked piercingly at Freddie.

"Let me show you something."

Freddie's fear was gone, replaced by a low burning anger as he stood in his brother's room.

His father had given it to Mr. Pheeps that first day they'd met him on the road, and the idea of someone else in here appalled him. He couldn't understand how his father had given up the room so readily, but he could see that this man had a way with words where his father was concerned.

The room contained a brass bed, a chest of drawers, and a little nightstand. The walls were yellow, and the carpet brown, and it always had a homely feel to it, a kind of charm.

But James was gone now, and even with two of them standing in the room it felt empty.

Mr. Pheeps nodded at his leather carryall.

"You've been wondering what's inside the bag, haven't you?"

Freddie straightened up and tried to hold Mr. Pheeps's gaze. "I haven't."

Mr. Pheeps grinned. He knew he was lying.

As Mr. Pheeps unzipped the bag, Freddie heard the delicate *clink clink* of glass on glass.

"They're all empty now," said Mr. Pheeps. "Well, except

for one." Mr. Pheeps held up an empty jar with a dirty yellow label. The letters on the label were slightly faded with age. "This one I found in Maldon in 1200 or thereabouts. It was pretending to be a sailor. How quaint." He put it aside and picked up another. "This one I found skulking in a bog in Ireland during the Famine. I found it very sustaining. Rather ironic really. But, as I said, all are now empty. Except for one."

He looked slyly at Freddie. "Would you like to see?"

Freddie's newfound courage seemed to be waning a little, but he steeled himself.

Mr. Pheeps took another squat jar from the bag and cradled it in his hands.

The jar seemed to contain a small glowing cloud, white at the edges, with a pulsing sapphire light shimmering at its heart. Looking at it made Freddie feel as if he were in a dream where everything felt right and was in its proper place, and there was nothing in the world but hope and love, and that was all that mattered. The shining light moved with a languorous delicacy, and it was beautiful and strange, and somehow Freddie knew it was alive.

"What is it?" he asked, his voice hoarse with terror and awe.

"A delicacy. Something that provides me with proper

sustenance. Indeed, a delicacy that, once consumed, might sustain me for a hundred years."

Freddie had no idea what he was talking about. He was still transfixed by the beauty of the cloud.

"I met her on a bridge in Budapest. I think it was sometime in 1888. It was a winter's night. Cold. Beautiful. Lit with stars. I'd sensed her in the city a few days before, and as is my habit, I waited. Waited for the right moment."

Mr. Pheeps held the jar up to his own face, and the blue-white light softened the cracks in his dreadful visage.

"She knew who I was the moment she laid eyes on me, but by then it was already too late. I hadn't seen her kind in eighty years. And I was hungry. So very hungry."

Mr. Pheeps closed his eyes, and a trembling took hold of his whole body.

"I've been saving her," he growled.

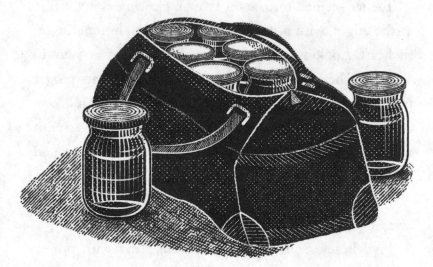

He uncorked the jar with quivering fingers, and Freddie almost screamed as Mr. Pheeps put the jar to his lips and opened his mouth. As his jaws opened wider and wider, it seemed as if the blue-white heart of light tried to back away toward the bottom of the glass, but there was no escaping its fate.

Her fate.

Freddie thought he heard something. It sounded like something fading just as you wake from a dream.

It sounded like screaming.

The light slipped into Mr. Pheeps's mouth. His lips closed around it, he gobbled it, chewed it, swallowed it down. For one horrific moment his throat ballooned like that of a bullfrog, the light pulsing blue underneath the skin, and then it was extinguished, and Mr. Pheeps's throat retracted.

The screaming stopped.

Mr. Pheeps tottered backward. He dropped the jar, which hit the floor with a *clunk* and rolled toward Freddie. Mr. Pheeps supported himself against the bed rail, gasping and licking his lips. He wiped a sleeve across his mouth and threw back his head and laughed.

"The thing is, you see, each time I consume one of them I become stronger. The problem is finding these creatures with the souls that burn so bright." Pheeps's face wrinkled into a sneer. "They call themselves the Family. They are such rare delicacies these days. And they hide so well, protecting themselves with their little sorceries, or hiding in ruins. I've had to ration the last two I found over the course of two hundred years."

Freddie picked up the jar. The letters on the yellowed label had faded with age.

"What was that?" he said, wiping his eyes.

Mr. Pheeps gave a deep sigh of satisfaction. His eyes seemed out of focus.

"That was proper food, boy. That was a living soul."

Mirabelle

"We're being watched," said Mirabelle.

They had just left the house and were making their way to the Path of Flowers. She could sense the birds above them in the dark sky. Their whirring wings and muffled caws occasionally punctured the silence. There seemed to be more ravens on the wall than she'd ever seen before: over a dozen, with more swooping down and landing silently with each passing moment. It was eerie to see them at night.

After spending time in the garden, she and Jem had returned to the house to wait for nightfall. Mirabelle could barely contain herself, knowing that they were heading to the village later. She felt excited, nervous, but most of all she felt defiant. Her excitement had grown as night drew in.

But then the ravens had started to gather.

It had started with some of them idly tapping their way along the roof at sunset. Then the one-eyed raven had started to flit erratically above the driveway, cawing madly, as if trying to attract attention. Eventually the other ravens joined him, wheeling about together before finally settling along the wall. They appeared to be waiting as she and Jem had made their way down the driveway.

"What are they doing?" Jem asked.

"They like to huddle together at night," said Mirabelle,

keeping her tone light. She was aware that Jem was nervous, and she didn't want her to feel any more frightened.

She didn't admit to Jem that she'd only ever seen the ravens huddle together during the day, and definitely not out here at night, not like this. She remembered Odd telling her once that he'd visited some cultures where ravens were portents of doom, harbingers of death.

Mirabelle put these thoughts to the back of her mind and decided to concentrate on keeping Jem as calm as possible, although she had to admit she was impressed with how Jem had handled things these last few days. She'd looked beaten down when they'd first met, but looking after her brother seemed to have made her stronger, and she now took the strangeness of the house and its inhabitants in her stride.

They'd left Tom in his room. He'd been resting again, and though he looked healthier, more at peace, he still needed to think about his experience with Piglet and try to take it all in. Whenever he and Mirabelle looked at each other, a silent understanding passed between them. Thanks to Piglet, they now understood each other in a way they never could have done before. She'd seen him at his worst. She'd seen him scrabbling for survival, taking beatings, stealing. There was no judgment on her part, and she could tell he was grateful for that.

Thinking about these things gave her strength.

But then she remembered that Piglet was still silent

and that the ravens were watching, and she felt the cold, creeping unease return.

She looked at Jem and tried to remember that she was with a friend.

"The tear is still there," said Mirabelle. "Uncle Enoch still hasn't found the right magic to close it, so until he does we can pass through."

"How far is it to the village?"

"Three miles, so I'm told," said Mirabelle, trying not to smile as she saw Jem's face drop.

Of course she could have asked Odd for help, but that would have meant risking his reporting her to Enoch, and besides, she wasn't entirely sure Odd was that comfortable with others traveling with him through his portals. The night they'd chased Piglet had been a unique case. Also, Odd seemed to be in the house even less now, and she wondered whether it had anything to do with the simple fact that he couldn't face her.

Good, she thought. *He should be ashamed. He has good reason to be. They all do.*

When they reached the Path of Flowers, Jem pulled up and stared at the spot where the driveway became a white chalk path.

"It's all right," said Mirabelle. "They won't touch you as long as I'm with you."

Jem nodded without taking her eyes off the path, and she pulled her cardigan tighter around herself. Mirabelle smiled encouragingly, and they both stepped onto the Path of Flowers.

Some of the flowers raised their heads and sniffed the air as they passed. Jem veered straight into Mirabelle. Mirabelle decided that the best way to deal with Jem's fear was to distract her.

"What was your mother like?"

She felt odd asking the question. Before her experience with Piglet, she wouldn't have considered the impact such a question could have. Now she regretted asking. The words seemed sharp, barbed, almost dangerous.

Fortunately, Jem looked grateful to be asked the question. "She was kind," said Jem. "Very kind, not like . . ."

Her brother, your uncle, Mirabelle thought, remembering the hulking shadow—that raised stick.

Jem shook herself. "She was just very kind, and she looked after us. She made us feel . . ."

"Safe," said Mirabelle, remembering her visions of Tom and how he'd felt before his mother had died.

Jem nodded. "She was a good person."

"Yes," said Mirabelle. "She was."

Jem frowned at her, and Mirabelle was about to explain what she meant, but she noticed something up ahead through the shimmering rip in the air. She raised a hand.

"Do you see that?"

Jem narrowed her eyes, looked straight ahead, then nodded.

She and Mirabelle crept up the path until they were a couple of feet from the tear. Mirabelle relaxed and chuckled when she realized what she was seeing.

"Come on," she whispered, waving Jem through.

They both stepped through the tear into the forest. A few feet ahead, muttering to himself and looking up into the night sky, was Bertram.

"Uncle?" Mirabelle whispered.

Bertram wheeled round and gave a high-pitched shriek.

"I wasn't doing anything bad," he gibbered. "I was just …" He pointed to the sky. "I was just looking … and … and …"

"It's all right, Uncle. We won't tell anyone. And we hope you won't either."

Bertram smiled gratefully, then looked startled when he realized what Mirabelle was admitting to. He pointed a finger at them agitatedly.

"You're not … you can't … ooh, but … ooh, this is …"

"Yes, Uncle?"

"You're . . . you're not supposed to be out here," he spluttered indignantly.

Mirabelle folded her arms. "Really, Uncle? And you are?"

Bertram hung his head. Mirabelle couldn't help but feel a warmth toward him. Only Enoch and Piglet were older than Bertram, but in many ways he was the child of the Family.

He waved his hands about. "I was just looking. It looks different, and it's been so long since I've been out here beyond the grounds."

He reached into his waistcoat, took out his notebook, and waved it and his pencil at Jem by way of explanation.

"I like experiences, you see. I like to record them. I like . . ." He looked up and pointed at the sky with his pencil. "This. I like how it's different to inside and . . ." He opened the notebook and started to flick through the pages. "I like to record the food I eat because I've never eaten like your kind have. I've never . . ."

Jem seemed genuinely intrigued, and she nodded for him to go on.

Bertram swallowed nervously. "I've never actually been able to taste your food, but I do like to . . . I like to try." He waved around him again. "And being out here . . ." He looked pleased with himself, then did a little nervous shuffle.

"Were you tempted to wander, Uncle?"

Bertram hunched his shoulders up and looked at the ground.

"What else were you thinking about when you were looking at the stars?"

Bertram looked bashfully at her. He shook his head.

"Were you thinking about Aunt Rula?" Mirabelle winked at Jem.

"No," he said, toeing the ground with a boot. "Maybe," he said, looking guilty.

Mirabelle felt an overwhelming urge to hug him, but she stayed where she was. The guilt came when she thought about what she was going to do next.

"You know you can't go looking for her?"

"I know that," Bertram snorted, scratching the back of his neck.

"And you know you shouldn't be out here."

"Neither should you," said Bertram, sounding like a petulant five-year-old.

"It would be terrible if Enoch were to find out you were out here," said Mirabelle.

"It would be worse if he knew you were out here," Bertram responded.

Mirabelle shrugged. "I'm already in lots of trouble, Uncle. It doesn't matter to me. Jem and I are going to the village."

Bertram looked shocked. "You can't do that," he whispered.

"We can and we will, Uncle. The only thing is, are we going to tell Enoch about what you've done?"

Bertram looked panicked. He fiddled with his cravat. Mirabelle felt genuinely terrible, but she'd seen an advantage and she was going to take it.

"You wouldn't. That's not fair," said Bertram.

"I wouldn't, but only under certain circumstances."

Bertram stopped playing with his cravat. "Under what circumstances?"

Mirabelle sighed. "Well, there is one thing . . ."

"What? What is it?" asked Bertram, his face twitching with hope.

Mirabelle smiled. "The village is three miles away, and it would be nice if we could get there and back before anyone notices we're missing."

Jem

Jem had never ridden on a horse before, let alone on a giant bear.

As they pounded down the road on Bertram's back, she could feel the muscles beneath his skin working like iron pistons. She held on to his fur as tightly as possible, and she marveled at how, with his loping run, it felt as if they were gliding between each footfall and then thudding against the earth only to rise again and glide . . .

Bertram had grumbled a little when Mirabelle told him what she wanted, but eventually he relented, only making one request: that Jem turn around while he "shed" his aspect and put on what he called his "proper one."

She already knew about Bertram's bear aspect, but Jem still marveled when she turned back round to see a ton of fur and claws and teeth and muscle standing before her. Bertram's red eyes glimmered in the night, and he lowered himself onto his forepaws, allowing Jem and Mirabelle to climb onto his back.

Before she knew it, they were away. The wind blew back her hair as they hurtled through the night, and she had to use all her might to stay on board. She was terrified but exhilarated, and she and Mirabelle laughed together when they glanced at each other.

Jem craned her neck up at one point and saw the stars. They were blotted out for a second, then reappeared and disappeared again. It took her a few moments to realize what she was seeing.

The ravens were following them.

Bertram slowed before the bend that would eventually take them into the village. He padded gently to the forest edge, and Mirabelle and Jem climbed off and stood just behind a tree. Jem was surprised at how disappointed she was to reach the end of their journey, and though she still felt a little giddy, she was already looking forward to the trip back.

Something across the road caught her attention, and she saw the one-eyed raven settle on a branch.

Mirabelle noticed it too. "Nosy," she said, scowling, and turned her attention back to the village.

Bertram sidled up to them in his human aspect.

"This is very bad. We shouldn't be doing this. It's forbidden," he hissed.

"Quiet, Uncle. If we do this properly, no one will know."

"This is very bad," he repeated, chewing on a knuckle.

Mirabelle took the first step toward the village. Jem's heart fluttered.

"Why can't any of you come to the village?" she whispered to Bertram.

"It's part of the Covenant, an agreement that goes back generations," he said, now chewing on his cravat. "No one from the Family may enter the village, and no one from the village may enter the estate."

"There are exceptions," said Mirabelle. "There's Mr. Fletcher, whose family has been bringing us meat for years. His father did it before him—"

"And his father before him, and his father before—"

"Yes, Uncle, I think Jem understands."

"And then there's Dr. Ellenby."

"He holds the key that allows Mr. Fletcher to open the way through the Glamour, which leads on to the Path of Flowers."

"Like his father be—"

Bertram stopped when Mirabelle frowned at him.

Mirabelle continued. "But the way in is no longer hidden,

thanks to the tear in the Glamour. He knows more than anyone about the matters relating to my family and the village. And he was there when I was . . ."

Jem noticed that Mirabelle seemed to be struggling with the idea.

" . . . born, I suppose."

There was an awkward silence. No one seemed to know what to say.

A raven flapped above their heads and landed on a branch. Mirabelle glared at it.

She turned to Bertram.

"Where is it, Uncle?"

"Where's what?" asked a bemused-looking Bertram.

"Where's Dr. Ellenby's house? I've seen you looking at the old maps."

Bertram turned to Jem. "I like looking at maps too. Maps are very interesting. When I'm looking at them, I like to find places I've never been and imagine I'm there and that—"

"Uncle!"

Bertram pointed to the opening of a lane at the end of a row of houses. "I think it's down there." The village was almost in total darkness, and Jem felt a tickle of fear and excitement.

"Right, then," said Mirabelle, waving them all forward.

They crouched low and headed in the direction of the houses.

The path was narrow. It stretched the length of four

derelict dwellings. Two of them were boarded up; two others had broken windows that yawned into the night. The lane was bordered by grass on either side and dipped in the middle, which meant it was wet underfoot because water had pooled in the channel. Jem's feet felt damp, but this wasn't too much of a problem. The problem was that the lane led to the entrance to the village green and continued again on the other side, which meant they would be exposed for a few moments.

They stopped at the mouth of the lane, and Jem could feel her neck and shoulders tighten with tension. Bertram pointed to the other end of the green and mouthed, "Over there." Mirabelle raised a hand, signaling them to wait.

Jem listened. She could hear the breeze and the distant bark of a dog, but nothing else. She was used to moments like this; she'd experienced so many of them while on the run with Tom, stealing about under cover of darkness. She'd almost forgotten what it felt like, and she was surprised to find that part of her had missed it.

"Low and quiet," Mirabelle hissed.

They broke cover and skirted the edge of the green. The village church loomed over the far side, dark against the night sky, clouds scudding past its spire, and Jem couldn't help but feel exposed beneath the starlight.

They made their way into the lane, which was longer on this side of the green. There was a grassy slope on the left, and they had to make their way past a row of terraced houses on the right. Bertram stopped, put a hand on Mirabelle's shoulder, and nodded at a door. A plaque beside it had DR. MARCUS ELLENBY, GENERAL PRACTITIONER engraved on it.

"All right," said Mirabelle, straightening up.

Jem noticed how she hesitated for a moment, as if not quite sure what to do next. Or maybe she was frightened by what she might discover. Jem looked at her encouragingly. Mirabelle understood her silent message and nodded in gratitude. She took a deep breath then knocked on the door.

A light came on in the hallway, glowing a warm gold in the arched window above the door. The door opened, and Dr. Ellenby stood there, blinking in astonishment.

"Mirabelle? Bertram? And Jem from London? To what do I owe the pleasure?"

"I have questions," said Mirabelle.

Dr. Ellenby nodded, stood to one side and waved them in. "Then I shall endeavor to answer them."

He led them through to his study.

"Would you like a brandy?" he asked.

Jem sat in a leather chair. There were framed photos on the mantle behind her, and bookcases lined three of the walls. Mirabelle sat in an armchair to Jem's left, while Bertram sat next to Mirabelle. Dr. Ellenby was behind his desk, holding up a bottle of brandy and a glass.

Jem was a bit confused about who the question was addressed to. The doctor's eyes twinkled with good humor as he noted her confusion.

"I meant, of course, those who are of an age to partake," he said.

Bertram raised a hand, and fished around in his jacket pocket before bringing out his notebook and pencil in readiness.

"How's Tom?" asked Dr. Ellenby while pouring some brandy.

"Good, thank you, Doctor," said Jem. She liked the doctor; he exuded warmth and reassurance. You only had to look at his eyes to see that he was a kind man.

"That's a relief. I hear he had a little experience with Piglet."

Jem wasn't sure what to say. Mercifully, Mirabelle interrupted.

"I had a similar experience, and I learned about some things, but I want to know more."

Dr. Ellenby regarded her for a moment as he passed the brandy to Bertram. Bertram snatched the glass with two hands, like an eager toddler grabbing a bottle of milk.

"Mmm," said Bertram, smacking his lips loudly. He'd already downed his brandy and was holding the glass out for a second tot. "That was . . . well, I think it was lovely. I'm not sure." He put the glass on the desk and started to open his notebook on his lap. "What would you say were the constituent elements of the flavor of this brandy? Might it share any similarities with, say, that of egg or, indeed, ice cream?"

Dr. Ellenby's eyes twinkled with amusement as he poured another brandy.

"I think perhaps, Bertram, that someone else here might have questions of a more important nature."

Bertram looked confused for a moment, then he glanced down the line at Jem and Mirabelle and wagged his pencil in the air.

"Ah, yes, of course," he said. He turned back to scribbling in his notebook.

Dr. Ellenby put his elbows on the desk and joined his hands together.

"Ask me anything, Mirabelle," he said.

"What was her name?" Mirabelle asked.

Jem noticed Dr. Ellenby's mouth twitch and the sorrow in his blue eyes.

"Alice. Your mother's name was Alice," he said quietly.

There was silence in the room, broken only by the reassuring ticking of the grandfather clock behind Dr. Ellenby.

"She was lovely," said Bertram in an awestruck whisper. "Dr. Ellenby thought so, didn't you, Dr. Ellenby?"

Dr. Ellenby closed his eyes and gave a sigh, and Jem knew that kind of sigh. She knew the pain of loss when she saw it. He opened his eyes again and tried his best to smile, but she could tell it was difficult for him.

"Yes, she was," he said.

"Enoch thought so too," said Bertram, raising his glass. "In fact, he was in love with her."

Dr. Ellenby plonked the brandy bottle in front of Bertram. "Take the bottle please, Bertram. Drink quietly, there's a good chap."

Bertram took the bottle gratefully and licked his lips.

"Enoch was in love with her?" said Mirabelle.

Jem noticed how completely still she was.

Dr. Ellenby took off his glasses and cleaned them with a cloth. "Yes, he was."

"I see," said Mirabelle. "I saw him when Piglet's mind touched mine. I saw lots of things. I saw you, Dr. Ellenby. I saw you on the Path of Flowers. I saw you because Piglet saw you. You were leaving the house the night my mother died."

Dr. Ellenby paused in cleaning his glasses. He put them on slowly and sighed, and now Jem saw the regret and grief in his eyes.

"Yes," he said hoarsely.

"She was beautiful," said Mirabelle. "What happened to her?"

"She died from blood loss during childbirth," said the doctor.

"Giving birth to me."

Dr. Ellenby shook his head. "Now you mustn't think like that, Mirabelle. It wasn't your fault."

Mirabelle nodded. "It wasn't yours either."

"That's what we kept telling him at the time," Bertram said.

"Where did she come from?" asked Mirabelle.

Mirabelle was poised, her back straight with tension as she waited for the answer.

"She came to the house for sanctuary, as some have done before. Except this time she wasn't one of the Family. She was human. She came to me first because she'd heard I was trusted by the Family, and so I brought her to the house."

"And Enoch let her stay. Why?"

Dr. Ellenby and Bertram exchanged a glance.

Dr. Ellenby tapped the table. "Because Enoch always felt responsible for those of his kind. Your mother was human, Mirabelle, but your father was a member of the Family. This meant you would be a member of the Family too. No one who is of the Family has ever been turned away."

Mirabelle nodded, and she frowned as she took in the information. "I understand. But tell me, who was my father? Where is he now?"

Dr. Ellenby threw up his hands. "Nobody knows. She rarely spoke of him. All she could tell us was that he was a member of the Family who had chosen a life in the human world. For all we know he may still be out there somewhere."

"And why did nobody tell me all this?"

Dr. Ellenby and Bertram exchanged another look.

"Because Enoch forbade it. He made a solemn promise to your mother to be your guardian and to look after you," said Bertram. "No one was allowed to tell you. I wanted to tell you, and Odd did too."

"But why did he forbid it?" said Mirabelle, her jaw clenched, eyes shining with anger.

"I'm sorry, Mirabelle. You'll have to ask Enoch that," said Dr. Ellenby. He leaned back in his chair, and Jem noticed how tired and old he looked, as if he'd just exerted himself by carrying a great weight.

Mirabelle looked at her hands in her lap. "Right, I see. But tell me, Doctor, and I'm asking you now in your professional capacity, can you help me?"

Dr. Ellenby leaned across the desk, his brow knotted with concern. "Of course, Mirabelle. What is it?"

Mirabelle looked up at him, her gray eyes cloudy with tears. She slapped a hand against her chest. "It's just that since I've learned about my mother I've been experiencing this pain. It comes and goes. And it hurts. It hurts so much."

Mirabelle lowered her head. Jem could feel the hot sting of tears in her own eyes, and she wiped them with her sleeve.

"I'm sorry, Mirabelle, but that's grief. It's something we humans experience. I'm afraid there's no cure for it," said Dr. Ellenby.

Jem felt a fierceness take hold of her. She was angry that Dr. Ellenby seemed so useless. The slack-jawed look of Bertram beside Mirabelle didn't help matters. She got up from her chair and held Mirabelle tightly. Mirabelle seemed surprised, but she returned the hug fiercely.

"It never goes away," Jem said, "but it does become less painful with time."

Mirabelle looked up at her. She seemed reassured and tried to smile. Jem squeezed her arm and sat back down.

"She's right, Mirabelle. It does," said Dr. Ellenby. "There is no cure, but time heals the wound."

Bertram nodded. "Yes, it does," he said. He looked quizzically at Dr. Ellenby. "Does it?"

Dr. Ellenby looked at the empty brandy bottle and sighed. "Oh, Bertram."

Mirabelle took a deep breath, straightened her back, and stood up. "We should go," she said.

Jem was impressed by her strength and poise.

Mirabelle reached a hand across the desk. "Thank you, Doctor. You've been most helpful. And kind."

She looked him straight in the eye, and he shook her hand and nodded in appreciation.

Bertram stood up, notebook in hand. "Carrot, perhaps? Does it taste of carrot?"

Dr. Ellenby raised his eyebrows at him.

"Goodbye, Bertram. I'm glad you enjoyed my brandy."

Dr. Ellenby escorted them all to the front door. Jem stole a quick glance at Mirabelle, and Mirabelle nodded to let her know she was all right. Despite her upset, Mirabelle seemed already stronger. Looking at her like this made Jem proud of her friend.

Dr. Ellenby asked Bertram whether the brandy had had any effect. Bertram shrugged. He looked clear-eyed and well aware of where he was. Dr. Ellenby made a remark about his "unique constitution" then wished them all goodnight. When the door closed, Jem and Bertram looked at Mirabelle.

"I'm going to talk to Enoch," she said. "I'm going to find out the full story once and for all."

"He owes you that much," said Jem.

"We should go," said Bertram.

They headed down the lane toward the green. A raven watched them, and Jem could see the moon glinting in its one good eye.

"Stop," Bertram hissed.

They all stopped as Bertram pointed at a figure sitting on a bench at the edge of the green. They would have to try to pass by whoever it was unseen, and Jem knew that was impossible.

She looked at Bertram. "Is there another—"

"It's all right," said Mirabelle.

Jem felt her heart lurch when Mirabelle stepped out of the lane, but she and Bertram followed, trusting Mirabelle's instinct.

"Freddie?" said Mirabelle.

Freddie looked startled. He'd been concentrating on something he was holding between his hands. He wiped his eyes, and it was clear to Jem that he'd been crying.

"You're not supposed to be here. It's forbidden," he said to them, but Jem could tell he said it more out of fear for their safety than as a warning.

"We're going back home straightaway, Freddie. We

promise. You won't tell anyone we were here, will you?" said Bertram.

Freddie shook his head and sniffed. "Course not."

"What's wrong, Freddie?" asked Jem.

She was startled when his face crumpled. "There's a man in . . . there's a man . . ."

Jem felt a sudden hot, prickling panic. They were standing in full view on the green, and she wanted to shush Freddie, but she didn't want to be unsympathetic.

"What man?" asked Bertram.

"A man who isn't a man," said Freddie. "He's some kind of . . . some kind of monster. My dad let him in. It's like he has him under a spell. He can't see that he's . . ."

Freddie's voice trailed off as he fought to compose himself.

"What's that you're holding?" asked Bertram.

Freddie held the object up. "It's a jar. He ate something from it. He said it was a soul."

Bertram tottered backward on his feet. For a moment Jem thought it was because he was drunk, but she remembered the brandy had had no effect on him whatsoever. This was something else.

"A what?" he whispered.

"A soul. He ate it. It was alive. She was alive. I'm sure of it. She was alive, and he ate her. And he says he hunts for these souls, and he's been hunting them for hundreds of years."

Bertram came toward him, his face twisted in fear. Jem exchanged a worried glance with Mirabelle. She could see she was disturbed too. The air was tingly, electric, and Jem felt the overpowering urge to run for cover.

"Give it to me," said Bertram, reaching out a hand. "Let me see it. Please."

The "please" was like something a child might say, an agonized plea, a yearning for protection just before the advent of some dire punishment. Jem's mouth felt dry.

"Uncle?" said Mirabelle, but Bertram didn't seem to hear her. His eyes were fixed on the jar.

"The jar. Please?" he said.

Freddie too looked concerned as he gazed up at Bertram, and he handed over the jar without taking his eyes off his face. Bertram took the jar and examined it. He turned it over in his hands and caught sight of the label.

That was when he scrunched his eyes shut and started keening.

Jem could see the terror in Mirabelle's eyes.

"Uncle? What is it? What's wrong?"

Bertram shook his head. "No, no, no!" he cried.

"Uncle? Please tell me."

He started to pound the jar against his forehead. "It has her name on it. It has her name on it," he moaned.

"Uncle, give it to me, please. Give it to me now," said Mirabelle, holding her hand out, trying her best to look in charge, but Jem could see the trembling in her legs that matched the trembling of her own.

Bertram went down on one knee, groaning like a

wounded animal. He handed the jar to Mirabelle. She looked at it, and Jem tried to read her face.

"What is it? What does it say?" she asked.

Mirabelle held the jar up for her to see. The letters were faded a little with age, but there was no mistaking what they said.

"Rula. It says Rula," said Mirabelle.

Bertram gave a hoarse, angry howl, and he punched the earth with his fist. Mirabelle let the jar slip from her fingers onto the grass.

Bertram sprang up and grabbed both Mirabelle and Jem by the shoulders.

"We have to go. We have to go *now*. It isn't safe here," he said.

He started to push them along.

It wasn't safe to begin with, Jem thought. *What makes it any less safe now?*

Freddie followed them. Bertram twisted his head round to look at him, his eyes wild.

"Where is he? Where is he now?" he barked.

"In my house," said Freddie, his face pale as they entered the second lane.

"Good," said Bertram, pushing both the girls in front of him.

A short, slightly portly figure was heading toward them from the other end of the lane.

"Mr. Teasdale," said Freddie.

Mr. Teasdale blinked in shock as he beheld them.

"What is this? What's going on?" he said, looking indignant.

Mirabelle stepped toward him. "We can explain, Mr. Teasdale, we—"

"You! You again! You're a troublemaker," he shouted, pointing his finger at her. "You're not supposed to be here. You know it's forbidden. I will report this grievous infraction to the council, and when they hear of it, your punishment will be doubled."

Mirabelle was standing right in front of him. "Please, Mr. Teasdale, you have to listen to us."

Mr. Teasdale pushed her out of the way with such force that Mirabelle collided with a wall. Jem felt a spark of anger, and she was just stepping forward when two black scraps of darkness plummeted from the night sky and launched themselves at Mr. Teasdale.

Ravens.

Mr. Teasdale squealed as they raked at his face. He batted at them with his hands, tripping over himself before crashing to the ground. Just as suddenly as the ravens had started their onslaught they stopped and flew off. Mr. Teasdale lay there, panting hard, righting his spectacles with a trembling hand.

"This will not stand! This will not stand!" he wheezed.

"No, it most certainly will not, Mr. Teasdale."

The voice came from a figure at the other end of the lane. It was a mellifluous voice, rich and melodic, seductive and powerful, but tinged with hate. Jem recognized the undertones.

The man stepped into view. He was wearing a battered old coat and had hair that was grayish brown. The most vivid thing about him was his smile. It was a smile that seemed a little too big and contained too many teeth. A smile of utter malevolence.

The man helped pull Mr. Teasdale up to standing.

"Why, thank you, sir," said Mr. Teasdale, blinking again, but now his eyes seemed slightly glazed.

"Not at all," said the man. "But take my advice for now."

"Advice?" said Mr. Teasdale almost dreamily.

"Yes, why not rest for a bit?"

The man clamped a hand to the back of Mr. Teasdale's head. Mr. Teasdale's eyes rolled up, and the man lowered him gently back to the ground as he fainted dead away.

The man turned back to Jem and the others, that smile still on his face. Jem had been frightened earlier, but now she was sick with fear. Her temples pounded, and she could feel her stomach roiling. She wondered if she had the strength in her legs to run. Mirabelle was by her side, and she could see that she too was terrified.

The man threw his head back and gave a great big sniff of the air.

"Oh my, oh my, what a wonderful scent that is. Heady

and sweet. You never told me about your friends, Freddie. You've been keeping secrets." He wagged his finger.

"Who *are* you?" Mirabelle demanded.

The man pretended to be shocked. "You mean you don't know?"

"I know," growled Bertram. "I know what you are."

Bertram was clenching and unclenching his fists. Jem could see he was clearly angry—angry and frightened. He was grinding his teeth. He was barely containing himself.

"I know what you did to Rula," he growled, his voice becoming deeper, his eyes darkening to a ruby red.

The man raised his hands in a gesture of innocence and shrugged. "But I was hungry."

It happened in less than a second. One moment there was Bertram. The next a ton of fur and claws exploded and hurled itself toward the man. Jem felt like roaring him on. In her mind's eye the man would become pulp.

In reality he sidestepped Bertram in his bear form, grabbed him by the haunches, and hurled him against the side of a house. There was the thud of brick, the tinkle of glass, the splinter of wood. Bertram slid down the wall, but was up on his haunches in seconds, shaking his shoulders and throwing his head back and roaring, baring his fangs to the night. He twisted round and launched himself at the man again.

This time the man didn't move. This time he simply caught Bertram by the scruff of the neck. Bertram twisted and roared, but he couldn't shake himself free.

A stunned Jem was vaguely aware that Mirabelle was gripping her arm.

The man turned Bertram round as if he weighed less than a kitten. Bertram's bear aspect started to melt and shimmer. His human form reestablished itself. He was sweating and twisting, trying to free himself, but the man held him in place with ease, an arm tight round his neck.

And now the man himself was changing form. His eyes became gray, his mouth widened. His fingers became talons. Jem was shocked, not just by the transformation, but by the terrible feeling that she had seen this creature somewhere before.

"I've been so hungry for so long," he said, his voice moist and bubbling.

Jem couldn't move. Freddie was backing away from the creature, shaking his head like someone desperately trying to rouse himself from a nightmare.

"Uncle?" Mirabelle cried.

Bertram tried his best to smile, but there were tears in his eyes.

"Run!" he said.

The creature bit down on his neck. Light bled from him, purple, red, fiery with life. The creature started to devour him, and as it fed, Bertram started to turn to dust.

Jem grabbed Mirabelle by the hand and ran.

The lane seemed to last forever. Jem stumbled, and Mirabelle pulled her up. They could hear the creature pounding after them. Jem could feel a terrible heat at her back, but she couldn't help herself. She turned around.

The creature slashed its claws through the air. Jem screamed.

She turned just in time to see Odd standing right in front of her, his face a mask of furious intent. He grabbed both her and Mirabelle and shoved them through a portal.

There was that rushing sensation again, and something else, as if something had raked the air behind her. Something hot and sharp. Jem fell onto grass. She looked up to see the house looming before her, Mirabelle on her knees by her side.

They both turned to see Odd walking toward them, the portal now a tiny black speck behind him. He smiled.

"Well, now, that was . . . that was . . ."

His smile faltered, and the color drained from his face. He reached behind him as if trying to scratch his back, then fell face-first onto the ground.

Piglet

Piglet screams.

He screams when he senses Bertram's essence leave his body. The moment is like a knife in his heart. Piglet screams and twists his head and thrashes around to escape the pain, but try as he might, he can't. The pain finds him. It fastens its teeth into him. The pain is raw and burning, and part of him knows he will never, ever escape it.

And after that moment, that horrible, pain-filled moment, there is something else. Piglet sees Mirabelle, the girl, and Odd appear in front of the house. He sees Odd stumble and fall. Mirabelle goes to him and holds him, and when she takes her hands away, they are wet and black, covered with Odd's blood. And now it is Mirabelle's turn to scream.

Piglet hides in a corner. And he weeps. He sobs. The hot, scalding tears come freely, and it feels as if they will never stop.

And now Piglet knows what grief is.

Freddie

Freddie ran.

He ran to escape the horror of what he'd just seen. He ran and he ran, but he was also running away from his own shame. He'd never felt so utterly helpless.

He arrived back at his house. He was just about to bang on the front door when he heard a voice.

"Freddie? What are you doing up and about at this hour?"

Constable Griggs was standing behind him. Freddie was panting. He tried to get the words out, but a shout of "Help!" distracted both of them.

Mr. Teasdale was limping up the street, supported by Mr. Pheeps.

Pheeps waved his hand. "Constable, please. This man needs assistance."

Griggs ran toward him.

"What happened?" the constable demanded.

"I was . . . I was . . ."

Mr. Teasdale looked confused. Freddie saw Pheeps whisper something to him. Only Freddie saw the man's grin.

"I was attacked!" Mr. Teasdale wailed.

His wail was enough to wake the rest of the street. Lights came on in bedroom windows. Freddie saw Kevin Bennett look out of his window, while Kevin's father came to his front door wearing pajama bottoms and a vest. His wife stood behind him in a fluffy blue dressing gown, her hair in curlers.

"What's going on?" Mr. Bennett shouted.

Constable Griggs went to Mr. Teasdale.

"Mirabelle of the House of Rookhaven attacked me!" Mr. Teasdale shouted.

"Is this true?" Constable Griggs asked Mr. Pheeps.

Mr. Pheeps nodded gravely. An enraged Freddie stepped forward, but a hand on his shoulder grabbed him and pulled him back. It was his father. He strode toward the constable and the two men, demanding to know what had happened. Mr. and Mrs. Smith were on the street now, and at least a dozen more people were venturing out of their houses, blinking and looking dazed.

"I was attacked!" Mr. Teasdale shouted again, and Freddie noticed how Mr. Pheeps kept a hand clamped on his shoulder, still whispering in his ear.

A crowd gathered around Mr. Teasdale, all jostling for position, demanding to know what the fuss was about.

"She transformed into a hideous monster, and she was in league with creatures who sought to injure me," Mr. Teasdale shouted, his eyes wide and strangely glassy, cheeks flushed.

"That's not what happened!" Freddie shouted, but no one heard him. The hubbub had increased in volume, and people were shouting. Freddie tried his best to be heard over the noise.

"I was there. That's not what . . ."

It was no use. No one was listening. Freddie watched in horror as Mr. Pheeps made his way among the people, touching some on the shoulder, whispering to others, and everyone he touched or spoke to seemed to cock their head as if listening to a far-off voice. Their eyes would first glaze over, and then their faces would harden with anger.

Freddie felt utterly powerless. Mr. Teasdale was still shouting, Freddie's father by his side. So many people were yelling now that it was hard for Freddie to hear exactly what was being said, but he caught snatches:

" . . . monsters . . ."

" . . . after all we've suffered . . ."

" . . . the ingratitude . . ."

" . . . they need to be taught a lesson . . ."

And in the midst of it all was Mr. Pheeps, smiling, cajoling, nodding sympathetically, patting people on the shoulder, working his strange subtle magic. To a helpless Freddie it seemed as if the people became one bristling, rage-filled entity, and all Freddie could think of was Mr. Pheeps's earlier words to him.

I'm just waiting for the right moment.

Part 4
Signs and Portents

Mirabelle

Mirabelle tried to focus on Odd's face as he lay in the bed, because she found that if she didn't, the image of Bertram's face caving in presented itself to her instead. She couldn't start crying again, not in front of Gideon, who had wrapped himself round her shoulders and refused to let go as soon as she'd entered the house.

Piglet had finally stopped screaming half an hour ago. She thought he was going to scream all night. Mirabelle would have gone to him, but she was too worried about Odd.

Odd's face was even more preternaturally pale than usual, paler than the sliver of moonlight that stretched from the window to his bed. At least his eyelids were flickering, she consoled herself. The time since their arrival back at the house had been a panicked blur. Eliza had met them at the door and helped carry Odd to a room, then dressed his wounds. Jem had suggested calling Dr. Ellenby, but Mirabelle had shouted, "What good would that do?" and immediately felt guilty when she saw the stunned look on Jem's face. Eliza had left the room, muttering something about talking to Enoch. Jem left moments later to find Tom. Mirabelle wanted to call after her, but she felt as if she were choking.

She wanted to shout at Enoch, who still hadn't made an

appearance. She wanted to scream at Eliza for seemingly running away. Round and round her anger went, until she thought her skull might explode.

Gideon squeezed himself against her neck. Mirabelle patted his arm and tried her best to smile, but it hurt. Everything hurt.

And all the time she saw Bertram turning to dust.

And that thing.

Its face. She'd seen it before.

"What was it?" she whispered to herself, and Gideon gave her a puzzled look.

Mirabelle reached out and held Odd's hand. She willed him to squeeze her fingers, but he was completely still.

The bedroom door opened behind her, and Jem stepped into the room, followed by Tom.

"How is he?" asked Jem.

"Still sleeping," said Mirabelle.

There was an awkward silence for a moment. Mirabelle looked at Jem.

"I'm sorry I shouted at you."

"That's all right," said Jem. "I understand." She reached into her cardigan pocket and took something out. "Here, I picked it up just before . . ."

Mirabelle took it from her. It was Uncle Bertram's notebook, battered and slightly muddy. The corners of its pages were curled up with age and damp, but to Mirabelle it was the most precious treasure in the world. She read the title he had scrawled on the cover: *Bertram's Investigations into the Tastes, Sights, Scents, Sounds, and Various Experiences of the World.*

Despite everything, it made her smile. "Thank you," she said.

"Will he be all right?" asked Tom, nodding at Odd.

Mirabelle wasn't sure what to say. "I don't know. This hasn't happened before—well, not that I know of." She frowned. "It seems there are lots of things that I don't know about."

The door opened again, and Eliza reentered. She walked over to Odd's bedside.

"How is he?"

"Better, I think," said Mirabelle, knowing she was trying to convince herself as much as Eliza.

"He'll be fine," said Tom, giving her a reassuring nod.

"Maybe, but for how long?" said Mirabelle.

She could see by the look in their eyes that they all knew what she really meant.

That thing is coming, she thought to herself. *And nothing can stop it.*

"Enoch is in the library," said Eliza.

"Well, we shouldn't keep him waiting, then," said Mirabelle, standing up.

She gently lifted a protesting Gideon from her shoulders. "Go to your room, Gideon."

Gideon squawked at her and swiped the air in anger.

Mirabelle shook her head at him. "Gideon."

Gideon snarled one more time, then vanished into thin air. There was a rattling, scampering sound, and the door opened, then slammed shut.

Tom whistled, looking impressed. "I wouldn't mind being able to do that."

Jem nudged him with her elbow. Tom looked suitably contrite, but there was still a trace of admiration in his eyes.

The library was bathed in candlelight and filled with the smell of wax and smoke. Enoch stood at the head of an oak table with a large black leather-bound book in front of him. Eliza went to stand with him. Dotty and Daisy stood to the side, both of them clasping their hands in front of them, their heads bowed. Sacred and peaceful as it felt, Mirabelle couldn't rid herself of the terrible ache when she remembered her mother and Bertram.

No one said anything for a moment. Mirabelle mentally dared Enoch to object to the presence of Jem and Tom, but he looked too tired to protest.

He opened his mouth to speak, but Mirabelle wouldn't let him. She had a question for him.

"That creature, the creature that . . ." She struggled to say the words. "I've seen its face before. It's carved on the door to Piglet's room. What is it?"

Enoch nodded, as if quietly conceding there was no point in hiding the truth anymore.

"We call it the Malice," he said.

There was a subtle change in the air, as if something had tainted it. Mirabelle noticed that Dotty had scrunched her eyes shut and was trying not to cry. Daisy stroked her arm and whispered gently to her.

Enoch opened the book, and Mirabelle stepped forward to look at it. The language was old and unfamiliar to her, the letters jagged and strange, as if someone had cut them into the yellowing pages in rage and pain.

"It is an ancient creature that has hunted our kind since we can remember."

Enoch turned the pages one by one. There were drawings of the same howling skeletal creature with long claws and sharp teeth pictured on the door to Piglet's room. One picture showed a man cowering in the foreground as the creature reared up before him against the night sky.

"For years the Glamour has hidden us not only from the humans, but also from the Malice. Alas, it now seems we have been discovered," said Eliza. Mirabelle could see that she was close to tears.

"The Glamour protected us, but with it damaged we were left vulnerable and open to discovery. The creature would have sensed Piglet when he escaped. Piglet has a very powerful essence and aura. To the Malice it would have been like a wolf catching the scent of its prey," said Enoch.

"How do we stop it?" asked Mirabelle.

Enoch wiped a hand across his brow and closed the book with a whumping sound.

"We can't," he said.

"What?" Mirabelle was incredulous. "Of course we can. That's just ..."

"We can hide," said Eliza.

"Hide?" Mirabelle roared. "*Hide?*"

Her anger was sudden and volcanic. It twisted up and through her until she could barely see.

"We're not hiding anymore! This thing killed Uncle Bertram. It killed Aunt Rula. It nearly killed Odd!" she shouted, pointing at the door.

She was panting hard, but all she got in response from Enoch and Eliza were sorrowful looks. They looked pathetic to her now. Pathetic and weak. She could see Bertram's face in her mind. She wiped a hand angrily across her eyes.

"This thing is a monster, and I say we kill it," she hissed

through teeth so tightly clenched it felt to her as if her jaw might break.

Enoch sighed. "We can only hide. The tear in the Glamour is almost healed. Once it's completely sealed, only the Family can pass through it. The only other way in is through the hidden entrance to the Path of Flowers. Even if the Malice does get in that way, the flowers are poison to him. There is no way he can withstand them."

"Then we send the flowers after him," said Mirabelle, slamming her fist against the table.

Enoch looked pained. "We can't command the flowers that way, and you know it. They are bound to their promise to protect the Family and the house. They provide a defense here, but no more than that."

"So that's it, then? We just wait for the Malice to come to us?"

Enoch nodded.

The agony of it all seared into Mirabelle's bones. The darkness seemed clammy and suffocating. She could hear the guttering of the candles and even that seemed to cause her pain.

"Everybody get out," she said.

Dotty and Daisy looked at each other. Jem took a step toward Mirabelle.

"Everybody except my beloved uncle, *get out*," Mirabelle growled.

Jem hesitated, then she and Tom both headed for the

door. Eliza and the twins looked at Enoch, who sighed and waved a hand at them in dismissal, then the three of them followed suit and left the room.

Mirabelle stared at Enoch. He seemed so much smaller to her now, and although she was angry with him, there was also a nagging hint of pity.

"Why did you do it?" she asked.

"The Malice wasn't something we thought you needed to know about."

"I'm not talking about the Malice. I'm talking about my mother. Why didn't you tell me about her?"

Enoch lowered his eyes and picked at a corner of the book.

"Enoch?"

He looked her in the eye again. "I had my reasons."

"Then tell me your oh-so-special reasons."

"I'm your guardian, Mirabelle."

"Of which you're so fond of telling me."

"As your guardian—"

"It was as good as a lie!"

Enoch looked suddenly furious. "I have never lied to you!"

"Only done much worse," Mirabelle shouted, shaking her head with contempt.

Enoch headed for the door. "I need to repair the Glamour. The incantation is almost complete, and there isn't much time."

"How often do you think about her?" Mirabelle asked, her voice surprisingly calm.

Enoch stopped in his tracks. He stood up straight and took in a deep breath.

"Uncle?"

He looked at her now, his eyes filled with sorrow. His voice was a hoarse whisper.

"Every day," he said, then left the room.

Mirabelle found Jem on the steps outside the front door. The night seemed darker than ever, but on the Path of Flowers an occasional burst of gold lit up the sky, then faded as if it had never existed.

"What is that light?" asked Jem.

Mirabelle sat beside Jem and nodded as another sliver of gold flared briefly then disappeared.

"That's traces of magic, apparently. I think Uncle Enoch finally found the right incantation and he's healing the tear. It should be mended soon," she said. She bit her lip. "It had *better* be mended soon. With the Malice out there . . ." She shook her head, unwilling to finish the thought. She decided to change the subject. "Where's Tom?"

"He went to talk to Piglet."

Mirabelle frowned at this.

"He heard him crying earlier, and he wanted to comfort him," said Jem.

"That's nice of him," said Mirabelle.

Jem laughed. "Nice. That's one word I never thought I'd hear said about Tom."

"He's always looked out for you," said Mirabelle.

Jem lowered her head. "I know. And I look out for him."

The one-eyed raven swooped down and landed on a pillar at the end of the steps. It cawed at them and fluttered its wings.

"I don't like you either," Mirabelle shouted.

The raven gave an almost dismissive flick of a wing and flew away toward the wall.

"There are more of them," said Jem quietly. "A lot more."

There were hundreds of ravens now, like a great liquid line of midnight black along the wall.

"What are they doing?" asked Jem.

"Waiting," said Mirabelle.

"What for?"

Jem looked almost sorry that she'd asked the question.

"Odd says that ravens are a dread portent of things to come. He says he's only seen flocks of them like that a few times before."

"Where?"

Now it was Mirabelle's turn to look perturbed.

"On battlefields," she said.

Freddie

Freddie watched as more and more people came outside. So many friends and neighbors. So many people who now looked unfamiliar to him.

Mr. and Mrs. Carswell were deep in discussion with the Smiths, their whispers hushed and intense. Mr. Pheeps moved among them, nodding and patting each on the back or an arm. Pheeps had even spoken to Alfie Parkin, and the cold dread Freddie felt became worse when he saw Alfie's face darken with anger. Now Alfie was standing there gripping his cane so fiercely his knuckles were white and sharp. Freddie waved to get his attention, but it seemed Alfie's mind was elsewhere as his eyes blazed into the night. For a while Freddie held tight to the hope that maybe the tide might turn and people would shake themselves of the insidious influence of Mr. Pheeps, but that hope was extinguished when he saw someone wielding a makeshift club and someone else cradling a rifle. Then he saw another gun.

And another.

It took him two minutes to get to Dr. Ellenby's house. As he pounded on the door, he could hear the low angry hum of people behind him, followed by a sudden, eerie silence that terrified him even more.

He fell over the threshold when Dr. Ellenby opened the door.

"Freddie? What's wrong?"

Freddie pushed his way in. "You have to go!" he shouted. "They'll be coming here."

"Who will?" asked Dr. Ellenby.

"Almost everyone in the village," said Freddie. "You must have heard them."

Putting his fear into words brought home to Freddie how dangerous the situation was. Dr. Ellenby frowned at him. Freddie grabbed his arm.

Freddie tried to catch his breath. "I think they're going to Mirabelle's house. I think they're going to do something terrible."

Dr. Ellenby considered all this for a moment, then nodded gravely when he heard the approaching buzz. It was distant, but there was no mistaking its rumbling, angry quality. He went into his study and took a set of keys from his desk drawer.

Freddie couldn't speak now. He was shuddering too hard. Dr. Ellenby came back to him and held him firmly by the shoulders.

"It'll be all right, Freddie. I know these people."

Freddie looked at him. *Not anymore you don't,* he thought.

Dr. Ellenby took him gently by the arm and guided him outside. He locked the front door behind them. Freddie could see the crowd approaching, spilling onto the green.

Mr. Pheeps was leading them, Freddie's father by his side. Freddie felt sick all over again.

The crowd squeezed into the lane, Mr. Pheeps looking extremely pleased with himself. Freddie's father stepped forward.

"We don't want any trouble, Marcus. We just came for one thing. If you can hand it over, we'll leave quietly," he said.

Dr. Ellenby frowned. "Trouble? There won't be any trouble here, Frank."

Mr. Pheeps put a hand on Freddie's father's arm and smiled at the doctor:

"Dr. Ellenby, I presume."

"At your service," said Dr. Ellenby. He started to address the crowd. "I know it's outside office hours, but if you could all just form an orderly queue . . ."

"Give us what we came here for," someone shouted from the crowd. More shouts followed, but they were silenced as Mr. Pheeps raised his hand.

"If you would be so kind as to do what's requested of you, Doctor, then we'll leave you in peace."

"And what *is* requested of me?" said Dr. Ellenby.

Mr. Pheeps stepped toward him, his hands held out in a gesture of placation. Freddie recognized the look on his face, the tone of his voice. It was the same hypnotic tone he'd used on his father. Freddie gripped the doctor by the arm.

"That's close enough," said Dr. Ellenby.

Mr. Pheeps looked surprised, and Freddie almost punched the air with delight.

"If you'd like to tell me what it is you came here for, well, then maybe I can oblige," said the doctor.

Mr. Pheeps closed his eyes and gave a long, hard sniff. "It seems this house has had quite a few visitors from a certain so-called *family*." At the mention of this a murmur of unease went through the crowd. When Pheeps opened his eyes again, the look he directed toward the doctor was one of pure malevolence.

"It would also appear that the way that was once open to a local property has now been closed. To gain entry to said estate would now necessitate the use of a certain *key*."

Mr. Pheeps held his hand out.

"If you would be so kind."

Dr. Ellenby pointed to the door of his house. "The key you seek is in there." He took a set of keys from his pocket. "And to gain access to the key that is in there, you'll need one of these."

He held the set of keys out, and Freddie's heart did a little flip. Mr. Pheeps stepped nearer, his eyes wide.

Dr. Ellenby brought his arm back and flung the keys with all his might across the lane into the darkness of the hedge beyond.

There was a collective gasp from the crowd.

Dr. Ellenby looked mildly at Mr. Pheeps, whose face was now contorted with rage. For a moment Freddie felt a little twinge of joy.

Then something flew out of the crowd and hit Dr. Ellenby in the temple.

The doctor staggered backward, using the windowsill behind him for support, but another stone hit him square in the forehead, and he crumpled to the ground, a hand going to his head and coming away covered in blood.

The crowd was on him in seconds.

Freddie tried his best to shield the doctor, but he was pushed out of the way, and then there was a flurry of fists and feet as the stricken man was pummeled by the crowd. Another group was battering the doctor's front door. They rushed it in waves, and about half a dozen men collapsed into the hallway as the hinges gave way. A great cheer went up, and people flooded into the house, which mercifully meant that they stopped attacking Dr. Ellenby.

Freddie tended to the doctor while the screaming crowd ignored them. Items were thrown from upstairs windows: shirts, shoes, books—all showering down around the doctor and Freddie. After a few minutes there was a frantic shrieking from the house, and someone came to the door, shouting:

"I have it!"

Freddie saw something golden held aloft, then the heaving crowd moved off as one, coursing like a river round the bend as they exited the lane. The silence they left behind almost hurt Freddie's ears. He helped Dr. Ellenby into a sitting position, noting the blood by his temple and on his forehead. His glasses were bent out of shape. The doctor tried to fix them back in place with a trembling hand.

"They're just scratches, nothing to worry about. Take it from me. I'm a doctor."

"What pitiable wretches you are," said Mr. Pheeps, regarding them from the darkness.

"Is that your professional opinion?" asked Dr. Ellenby as Freddie helped him to his feet.

"What good did it do you to resist?" asked Mr. Pheeps, shaking his head in disbelief.

"Good was done by the act of resistance, as futile as it might have been. That's all that matters," said Dr. Ellenby, pulling briskly at the hem of his waistcoat as he straightened himself up.

Mr. Pheeps shook his head in disgust and walked after the crowd.

"You'll get what's coming to you!" Freddie roared after him.

"Oh, believe me, I intend to," shouted Mr. Pheeps without turning round.

Jem

Jem and Tom stood at the bedroom window. They looked out across the estate to the wall where the ravens still gathered in preparation, for what exactly Jem didn't know. It was something she didn't really want to consider.

"We should help them," said Jem.

"I agree," said Tom.

Jem looked at him in surprise. Normally, Tom would run at the first sign of trouble. Their life on the road had always been about survival, taking what they needed wherever and whenever they could, and leaving as quickly as possible. Even so, she knew there was good in him.

"You can thank Piglet," said Tom. "He showed me things, made me understand how people are afraid of each other without having any reason to be." Tom frowned a little, as if the words he was trying to find were inadequate for the task. "We have more in common with this family than we think. Piglet is kind, and his family are kind, and we owe them."

"We're staying, then," said Jem.

"Absolutely," said Tom.

There was a knock on the door. They both turned as it opened, and Eliza stepped into the room.

"They're coming," she said.

Freddie

Freddie tried his best to support Dr. Ellenby as they entered his house. It required some effort, and Dr. Ellenby groaned.

"Does it hurt?" asked Freddie.

Dr. Ellenby gestured at the clothes, books, and furniture scattered around. "Only my aesthetic sensibilities," he said, giving a pained smile.

Freddie didn't fully understand what he meant, but he nodded anyway.

Dr. Ellenby fell into a chair in his study. He took some cloth and bottled spirits from the side table and wiped the gashes on his face, wincing as he did so.

"This Mr. Pheeps, what is he exactly?"

"A monster," said Freddie. "He eats souls. The souls of people like Mirabelle and her family. He says he's been hunting them for years."

"I see."

"His words have some kind of power. He can turn people against each other. I saw him do it to my dad first."

Dr. Ellenby nodded as he taped some gauze to his forehead.

A vehicle pulled up outside, and the window glowed orange from the headlights before they were extinguished. Freddie immediately stood up and clenched his fists.

"More of them," he said.

He looked around for a weapon, but Dr. Ellenby grabbed his hand, shaking his head. Freddie was about to protest when he heard someone call his name.

He was already rushing to hug his mother before she entered the room.

"Mum! Mum! Dad and the others, they're headed to—"

"The house, I know."

"We have to stop them!"

His mother's eyes were lit with a fierce light. "I agree. That's why we're going after them."

It took a little longer than normal for Dr. Ellenby to get his aching frame into the van. He collapsed gratefully into the passenger seat. Freddie sat beside him, noticing how weary he looked. He patted him on the arm.

"We'll stop them, Dr. Ellenby."

Dr. Ellenby tried his best to smile. "I don't doubt it, Freddie."

It was the first time Freddie had seen his mother drive the van. She crouched over the steering wheel, driving with an intent and purpose that surprised him. They pulled up when they saw the various cars and vans blocking the road. They could see the glimmer of torches between the trees and, most disconcertingly of all, the flicker of flames.

Freddie's mother stopped the van, and she and Freddie got out. She tried to object as Dr. Ellenby began to clamber out too.

"Well, why'd you bring me, then? And surely, Elizabeth, I am best qualified to judge whether I can do this or not."

Freddie's mother relented. The two supported him as they made their way through the trees. Freddie pointed the way. He'd traveled here countless times before. They stepped into a small clearing to be confronted by the sight of the townsfolk gathered around Mr. Pheeps and Freddie's father, some of them carrying makeshift torches. The smell of oil and burning rags made Freddie want to retch. Freddie's father was holding the circular key against his chest while he stood looking down at the pillar. He looked desperately unsure of himself, and Freddie thought he saw a glimmer of anger in Mr. Pheeps's eyes.

"Well then, Mr. Fletcher. Let us commence. I'm sure you're well versed in the procedure."

Freddie's father held the key just above the grooves on the pillar. Freddie could still see the doubt in his eyes. His hand was trembling. He laid the key in place, pausing before turning it.

"Dad! Don't!" Freddie shouted.

Mr. Pheeps whipped round to snarl at him, but soon forgot him as the air began to crackle with what felt like invisible sparks. A sudden swirling vortex of rainbow colors formed at head height above the throng. The colors ran together, and the people took a step back in awe as everything flared to a brilliant brightness. They covered their eyes as one.

The light vanished.

Everyone opened their eyes again to be faced with what could only be described as a gap in the world, a tall rectangular window looking into the small pocket of reality that was home to the Family. They could see the white snake of a path and the walled estate up ahead.

No one said anything for a moment. Even Mr. Pheeps was struck dumb. He started to pant. Freddie saw his eyes flicker to gray. He licked his lips and clenched his fists, then he threw back his head and gave a guttural, demonic howl.

The townspeople took this as their cue, and together they charged up the path.

The flowers were waiting for them.

Mirabelle

Mirabelle held a hand to her stomach. She'd been watching from the steps of the house with some of the others, and she'd felt an almost physical pain seeing the Glamour breached. She presumed it was fear she was feeling. Of all the things she'd witnessed recently, this was by far the worst because she knew it was possibly the end of everything.

Gideon was by her side, one hand wrapped round her leg. She heard him gasp.

"I told you to go inside," she hissed at him, and then felt immediately guilty when she saw the way he looked up at her so helplessly.

"Now!" she snapped.

Gideon mewled, let go of her leg, and vanished from sight. Mirabelle immediately felt stung by his absence.

Jem and Tom and Aunt Eliza stood alongside her, while Enoch flew above the estate wall for a closer view. It had been his idea to send the younger flowers out as a second line of defense. They had been only too willing to join the fray, and Mirabelle had watched with a mixture of pride and fear as they crawled down the driveway on their roots, hissing and snarling as they went. They were as much part of the Family as anyone, she reckoned. They had just as much right to defend their home.

She tried to calm herself, taking deep breaths. Jem grabbed her hand and squeezed.

And all the while the ravens watched, their feathers bathed in moonlight and flame.

The sight of them only made Mirabelle feel worse.

Freddie

The path was a vision of chaos as the flowers shrieked and snapped at the invaders. People thrust their flaming torches at the plants, and the night air became rent with moist, high-pitched squeals of pain as the flowers burned. Others used their guns, and green flesh plumed in the sky as bullets found their mark. The flowers tried to rally, but the fierceness of the onslaught took them completely by surprise.

Freddie saw Alfie Parkin flailing at the flowers with his cane. He saw a hysterical Mr. Teasdale, weeping and gibbering, slashing at one flower with what looked like a poker. Mr. and Mrs. Smith were both wielding sticks. To Freddie, each and every one of his fellow villagers looked possessed.

Freddie couldn't help himself. He followed, keeping one eye on his father the whole time. His father walked with the dull, loping gait of a man in a trance, seemingly unable to take in what was going on around him. Unlike the others he didn't attack the flowers. Freddie's mother called after Freddie, and he was dimly aware of Dr. Ellenby limping after him and trying to restrain him, but Freddie was compelled forward. He had to get to his father. He had to try to break the spell. He grabbed his father's hand.

"Dad! Dad!"

His father turned on him, his eyes suddenly blazing.

"Go back, boy!" he shouted, and pushed Freddie to the ground.

Freddie landed hard and saw the look of panicked guilt in his father's eyes.

"Go back," he sobbed. Then he turned and followed the mob.

Freddie got up and dusted himself off, gripped by a new fierceness. He followed the crowd and didn't flinch as they blasted the flowers, stabbed at them, set torches to them. His eyes focused on one figure, that of Mr. Pheeps. The mob had formed a protective horseshoe around him, keeping him from the reach of the flowers.

His mother grabbed him by the arm. He wheeled round to her and pointed at Mr. Pheeps.

"Look at him, Mum. He's just a coward. He's using everyone else to save his own skin."

The shrieking of flowers had died down. Now there was only the odd sickening thud and dull grunt as people battered the last remaining few to the ground, and to Freddie that somehow seemed much worse.

Mirabelle

Mirabelle was crying, but they were tears of rage. She watched the devastation wrought on the Path of Flowers and felt utterly helpless.

"I think that's nearly the last of them," said Tom, his voice hoarse and low.

Mirabelle looked to where Eliza had been standing only a few moments ago. She wiped her tears viciously with her hand. She could hear roars of victory rising up from the path.

"Doesn't matter," she said defiantly. "Time for the next line of defense."

Freddie

Freddie was revolted by the fury and savagery of the villagers. The victory roar that went up from them was even more sickening. His mother was crying, and Dr. Ellenby looked stunned by the devastation.

Mr. Teasdale was standing over the squirming body of a flower as it hissed and rattled, breathing its last. He raised the poker above it, ready to plunge it through the flower's soft flesh.

"Mr. Teasdale!" Freddie's mother roared in disgust.

Mr. Teasdale blinked for a moment, like a man suddenly roused from a dream. He appeared dazed, and a look of shame eventually crossed his face. He let the poker drop by his side, then turned from the flower and joined the throng gathered before the gate.

Mr. Pheeps was clapping.

"Very well done, very well done. You are all to be congratulated."

People were breathing hard, the night air fogging with their breath. Each of them seemed half-asleep, as if caught between waking and dreaming. Freddie saw his father look at his own hands with incomprehension.

"They did well," said Pheeps, turning to Freddie and the others.

Freddie glared at him.

Mr. Pheeps clasped his hands together gleefully.

"This is your moment—there is nothing to stop you now! Exact your punishment—"

"I think Eliza might have something to say about that," said Dr. Ellenby, pointing.

Between the two stone pillars of the gate a black cloud rose up, hissing and roiling.

Mr. Pheeps laughed. "I very much doubt tha—"

The cloud rolled forward with impossible speed and broke up into its constituent parts. The villagers found themselves confronted with a wave of thousands of spiders.

Mr. Teasdale shrieked as the mass of spiders spun up his legs, covering his body in a fizzing layer of black. He danced about and flapped his hands, trying to dislodge the spiders, but they held fast.

Most of the villagers found themselves dealing with the same problem. Freddie watched in delight as Constable Griggs batted at spiders with his helmet, while Mr. Carswell pitched headfirst into a hedge, his face covered with the creatures.

Mr. Pheeps screamed at the people, urging them to pull together in the face of Eliza's attack.

Freddie felt a small twinge of hope. Dr. Ellenby put a hand on his shoulder.

"She's just buying them some time," he said.

Jem

Jem watched in admiration as Eliza attacked the villagers. A small part of her hoped that they would be forced to turn back, but she knew it was a vain hope.

Eventually the wave of spiders pulled back, like a black tide heading away from a shore. The people were still reeling, so Eliza had time to reconstitute herself as she made her way back up the driveway, but she was limping. Mirabelle's aunt reached the steps, and Jem's heart lurched when she saw the gaps in her face. Even so, Eliza tried her best to smile. She sat on a low stone pillar to rest and regain her strength.

"She did very well," said Odd.

Jem jumped with fright. Odd had appeared by her side, and he smiled when he saw the look of astonishment on her face.

"I know what you're thinking, but appearances can be deceptive," he said. "I walked here." He frowned. "Although 'crawled in complete agony' might be a more apt description." He turned to Eliza. "You did very well, Aunt. We're all very proud of you."

Eliza raised half a hand weakly in salute.

Odd winced and held his side.

"You shouldn't be here, Odd," Mirabelle said.

"Where else would I be except here to watch the

destruction of a centuries-old dynasty to which, I reluctantly admit, I have at times been proud to belong."

"You're very convincing, Odd," said Eliza wryly.

He stumbled slightly, and both Jem and Mirabelle caught him. He tried to smile.

"I know what you're both thinking. The situation is dire, and perhaps Odd can do something, but I confess I am too weak, and even if I could transport everyone, that thing would eventually find us."

They all turned to watch as the crowd slowly began to recover. Silhouettes by the gate picked up weapons they'd dropped in the panic, readying for their next advance.

Nobody said anything. Jem felt sick with fear. She looked at Tom for reassurance, but he was staring grimly ahead. Her mind was spinning. Surely there was some way they themselves could help. All she'd seen was pain and destruction and violence, and there didn't seem to be anything to counter it.

Except . . .

She turned and went into the house. Mirabelle called after her, but Jem shouted back over her shoulder and said she would return as quickly as she could. She found the twins in the hallway, peering fearfully out the window. She tried to grab one by the shoulders, feeling foolish when her hands went right through her.

"Dotty, I need your help. I want you—"

The girl pointed at the other twin. "That's Dotty, I'm Daisy," she said, looking disgusted.

"Sorry," said Jem. She turned to Dotty. "Dotty, I need you to get the key to Piglet's room and meet me there as quickly as possible."

Dotty looked terrified. "I can't do that. Enoch will be angry."

Daisy rolled her eyes. "Just do it, Dotty. It probably won't matter very soon."

Dotty looked unsure for a moment, then nodded.

Jem didn't waste another second. She ran as fast as she could down into the depths of the house, to the eerie silence of the corridor outside Piglet's room. She was both relieved and terrified when she saw Dotty already waiting for her. Dotty pointed at the ceiling.

"I got the key from upstairs then I took a short cut."

Jem gratefully took the key and inserted it into the lock. She took a deep breath and turned it. There was a dull, heavy clank as she felt the lock give. She looked to her left, but Dotty was gone. She grabbed the door and pulled it open. It wasn't as heavy as she'd thought, but she was panting now, more from fear than exertion. She strained her ears to hear, both what might be going on outside as well as within Piglet's room.

There was nothing but silence.

She crossed the threshold, feeling the cool damp air on her face, her arms outstretched as she tried to feel her way. She inched forward slowly. She couldn't see anything, but the space before her seemed somehow vast.

"Piglet?" she whispered, her voice echoing in the darkness. There was no response.

"Piglet? Are you there?"

She thought she heard something like a low, quiet moan.

"Piglet? Is that you?"

Something lumbered past her in the dark, and her heart started to pound. She closed her eyes and swallowed.

"Piglet, please, we need your help."

There was another moan.

"Your family needs you, Piglet."

This was greeted with a groan. It was a weary sound, filled with a sense of defeat.

"I know you miss Bertram."

Something huge suddenly thrashed about in the dark, and there was a great clanging followed by a bellow of pain and anguish. Jem froze.

"Please," she whispered again. "Your family needs you."

There was nothing but silence now. Jem waited. The silence stretched on and on. With each passing moment the faint stirrings of hope she'd felt when she hit upon her idea started to fade. She shook her head and started to turn toward the door. She could feel the telltale sting of approaching tears. She stopped and shouted, "*Mirabelle* needs you!"

There was the sound of something like a great unfurling of wings, the grand movement of a giant fin in the depths of the ocean, panting like the hot breath of a dragon. Then two red eyes suddenly blazed in the dark.

Mirabelle

The fear. The pain. It was almost crippling now. Mirabelle watched as the villagers gathered for one final assault. She could see the Malice in the center of the crowd, and she knew this was the end.

A shadow passed over, and seconds later Enoch landed beside her.

Enoch frowned at Odd. "You should be resting."

"Thank you for your concern, Uncle, but I suspect I may be of more use here. We need all the help we can get." He looked at Tom, who was holding a piece of wood.

Tom, looking slightly embarrassed, held up his makeshift weapon. "I thought I could help."

Enoch gave him a sharp nod, which Mirabelle recognized as a sign of deep gratitude. She managed a rueful smile.

Enoch stood stiffly beside her, unable to look at her.

"What is it, Uncle?" she asked.

"Nothing," he said, staring at the advancing crowd, a muscle in his jaw flickering.

"Uncle?"

He looked down at her, and she was shocked to see tears welling in his eyes.

"They die, you see, the mortals. They die, and their loved ones experience pain. I wanted to save you from that. The pain. If I'd told you about your mother, it would have hurt you the way I've seen it hurt them. I only wanted to protect you from that."

Mirabelle took his hand. "Thank you, Uncle, but you didn't have to."

"I'm your guardian. I made a promise to your mother."

Mirabelle squeezed his hand. "It's better that I understand the pain."

Enoch nodded.

They both turned to face the crowd. The Malice was at its head, and it was smiling.

Freddie

Freddie was talking to his father, trying to keep in step with him.

"You know you don't have to do this, don't you, Dad?"

Tears were streaming down his father's face. His lips were moving silently, his eyes fixed on the house. They were only a few feet from the steps. Freddie could see Mirabelle and Odd, Enoch and Eliza. The twins were looking out a window.

"Dad?"

Mr. Pheeps's voice rang out. "And lo, so it came to pass that the good people of Rookhaven freed themselves from their shackles."

His eyes were gleaming, and to Freddie he looked more loathsome than ever.

"Now if you people would be so kind as to move forward and ensure that these *people* receive their just deserts."

The crowd advanced with purpose. Freddie could see Mirabelle and the others just standing there waiting. He wanted to shout at them to run. Why didn't they just run? The crowd was so close to them now. They would be upon them in moments and then . . .

Freddie didn't want to think about it. He held his breath. A line of men had already reached the foot of the steps. They were already raising their weapons.

Then the doors of the house exploded outward in a shower of splinters as something huge and black burst through the door. It reared up on its hind legs and bellowed at the night sky. Freddie could barely take it in. It had dozens of green eyes, or perhaps they were orange, all made of a beautiful liquid fire. It had a ruffle of scarlet feathers, and it was horned and taloned like some mythical beast. It bellowed

again, and the crowd started to scatter in terror as it pelted directly toward them.

"KILL IT! KILL IT!" Mr. Pheeps screamed.

Freddie heard Mirabelle shout, "Piglet! No!"

Piglet! That creature was Piglet!

Mr. Pheeps was still screaming.

"KILL IIIIIIIIT!"

A half-dozen "brave" souls raised their weapons. Through some miracle they all fired at the same time.

And, right in front of Freddie's eyes, Piglet exploded.

Piglet

Piglet was frightened when the girl came to him.

He wanted her to go away. He'd been frightened for a while now. It felt as if he'd been frightened forever. It felt like that because Piglet had never been frightened before the Malice came. The fear hurt. It hurt every part of his being.

And he missed Bertram.

And he was afraid for Odd.

There was so much fear and pain.

The girl begged him to help, but what could he do? The creature that had killed Bertram was not something that could be beaten. Piglet knew that.

Then the girl had asked him to protect Mirabelle. And he thought about Mirabelle, and how much her voice meant to him. How much having her near meant to him. And he thought about the creature and how it wanted to hurt her. How it wanted to hurt all of them.

And for the first time in his life Piglet knew rage.

And now here he is, facing the creature, facing the people from the village.

He hears the creature scream. He likes the sound because he hears fear in it. He sees the people look at him, the terror in their eyes, and he pities them. Even the ones who fire their weapons at him.

And Piglet explodes.

He explodes into dozens of shining golden lights, and each light flies through the night air and finds its mark.

Each light finds a person.

Each light is Piglet.

And as each light enters a person, they know Piglet and he knows them.

He knows Mr. and Mrs. Smith. Knows how Mr. Smith goes to bed late each night after he weeps in front of the fire over his two sons because the tears always come at night and he is afraid of his wife seeing them. Mr. Smith wants to be strong for her. He wants to protect her. But Piglet knows Mrs. Smith now too. He knows how much she loves her husband, and how seeing his tears won't hurt her but will help her in some way, because then they can share the pain, carry the burden together.

Piglet knows Alfie Parkin too. Knows how freakish and ugly Alfie feels. How every week Alfie goes into the bakery to buy a pastry from Amy Nicholson because he likes Amy and thinks she has a nice smile. He knows too how ashamed Alfie feels when he leaves the bakery, because even though talking with Amy makes him feel lighter, he always remembers who he is when he leaves, how useless he feels, how ugly. And he goes home and throws another pastry in the bin.

And Piglet knows Amy too. He knows that she likes Alfie Parkin. She likes Alfie Parkin a lot. But Alfie will only chat to her for a few moments, and then it is as if a cloud passes over his face, and he remembers something terrible. Then Alfie leaves the shop. And Amy feels that there is something between them, an unbridgeable chasm that will always be there, and she doesn't know how to cross it.

And Piglet knows Mr. Teasdale and how he likes his collection of clocks and how his cat means the world to him, and how he is afraid and nervous all the time, and how he hides this by pretending to be constantly angry. He knows Constable Griggs and how much his job and honor mean to him. He knows the Bennetts and the Carswells . . . He knows so many of them.

He knows the Fletchers now too. He knows of the terrible oppressive weight of the loss of James and how it has come between them, how they can't talk about it. He knows that Freddie desperately wants to reach out to his father, but doesn't know how. He knows that Freddie's father is afraid of expressing love for his one remaining son because he has already lost one, and to tell another he loves him would be to risk too much, so Mr. Fletcher has gathered around him a hard carapace to protect himself, and yet that carapace also hurts. He knows how much Mr. Fletcher's wife wants to reach her husband too, but for all her gifts she doesn't know how.

But Piglet watches them now. Because now they know one another, and he sees Freddie move toward his father. His father is crying, and Freddie hugs his father, and very soon the whole Fletcher family is embracing, and they weep together, and Piglet weeps with them, but his weeping is tinged with joy.

This is what Piglet sees as he passes through the minds of the people of Rookhaven.

And as they pass through his.

And as their minds touch they all know one another. They know their frailties, their weaknesses, their fears, and in this way they are all revealed. And the hatred the Malice has sown in all their hearts melts away.

Piglet leaves them now. But he carries a part of each of them with him. He knows each part is a gift.

And the people of the village are themselves again.

And thanks to Piglet they are free.

Mirabelle

Mirabelle watched as the dozens of golden lights into which Piglet had transformed left their hosts and floated up into the air to form a fine golden mist, pulsing with splashes of rainbow color. The mist then glided back in through the front door of the house to return to Piglet's room. She felt relief flood through her, knowing that Piglet was safe.

Most of the people had collapsed to their knees. She saw the Fletchers holding each other, saw the dazed looks on everyone's faces. Some people were crying.

The Malice screamed at them.

"Get up! Get up, you fools!"

But no one was listening. Some people staggered up and helped their friends. Not one of them paid the Malice any heed.

Odd nudged Enoch. "Piglet is dangerous, eh?"

Surprisingly, Enoch allowed himself a ghost of a smile.

"It worked," gasped Jem, running up to Mirabelle.

"How did you know?" asked Mirabelle.

Jem shook her head. "I didn't. It was a guess. I knew what he could do. Tom told me, and I thought if they could all see each other as they really are ..."

The Malice was still screaming. It clenched its fists in frustration, then turned to look at the Family.

"No matter. I can finish the job myself."

Mirabelle felt her stomach lurch as the Malice advanced toward them. Jem grabbed her arm.

They were both almost knocked off their feet as Enoch took flight. Mirabelle punched the air and bellowed as he landed on the Malice and sent it flying into the dirt. People scattered, but the Malice was on its feet in seconds, and as Enoch launched himself at it again the Malice sidestepped, and a claw flashed through the air and took Enoch in the wing. Now it was Enoch's turn to hit the dirt, and he tumbled over and over, attempting to form a protective cocoon with his wings, but Mirabelle could see that one was twisted back as if broken.

Mirabelle started down the steps, but Jem pulled her back, mouthing the word "no."

Enoch lay on the ground. He tried to raise himself up, but fell back. The Malice loped toward him, smiling. Its smile vanished when Freddie stepped between it and Enoch. The Malice halted, cocking its head in surprise. Freddie was joined by his mother, then his father. A bedraggled but defiant-looking Mr. Teasdale followed and stood with them. Gradually more of the villagers followed, all of them forming a barrier between the Malice and Enoch.

"Don't you dare take another step," said Freddie.

The Malice looked at Enoch's would-be rescuers with mild astonishment, then it doubled over as it burst out laughing.

"Oh my. It seems the useful idiots have found a new purpose. How utterly marvelous."

It straightened up, wiping tears of laughter from its eyes. Freddie glared at it.

"Is this the best any of you can offer?" the Malice jeered.

"We won't give up without a fight," Mirabelle shouted.

The Malice shook its head and smirked. "Oh, but you will." It suddenly sniffed the air and looked into a tree just above him. Mirabelle could see the leaves moving, and she looked around her at the others standing on the steps and realized something with a sickening clarity.

"No," she shrieked.

It was too late. The person in the tree leaped at the Malice, screaming in rage. The Malice was surprised only for a second, then its claws closed around thin air and its mouth widened.

Mirabelle ran down the steps toward the Malice as Gideon materialized in its claws. He was slashing the air with his hands, biting and snapping in an effort to reach the Malice. The Malice laughed at him.

"You're a feisty little one, aren't you?" the Malice sneered.

It sniffed the air just above Gideon's head. "And brand-new too. You'll be nice and fresh. Lovely and sweet. I might save you till last."

It wagged a clawed finger as it caught sight of Mr. Fletcher taking a step toward him. "Now, now, Mr. Fletcher. I wouldn't if I were you." It waved the same finger back and forth across Gideon's neck. "There's no telling what I might do."

Freddie laid a hand on his father's arm, and Mr. Fletcher took a reluctant step back.

"Put my brother down," Mirabelle growled. Her heart was pounding, and it seemed to her that the whole night was throbbing with pain. The ache within her was worse than ever, becoming steadily stronger as the night had progressed.

The one-eyed raven dropped from the night sky and landed on her right shoulder.

The Malice nodded at it. "He knows. He knows what you are. You're carrion. Meat only fit to be eaten by crows. Isn't that right, Mr. Raven?"

The raven glared at him.

Mirabelle's breathing became steadier. She looked at the raven, and it cawed at her. She had felt oddly serene as soon as it had landed on her shoulder. As if it felt . . .

The Malice sniffed the air again. "You're an odd one," it said to Mirabelle. It sniffed again. "You don't smell right, you smell . . . *different.*" It shrugged. "No matter. Like I said. Carrion."

Its mouth started to grow. Its eyes misted, grayed over, and bulged. Its claws elongated, and Mirabelle could see its teeth sharpen and multiply. The ache within her was insistent now. Gideon squirmed, but the Malice had a firm grip on him, and it brought him closer and closer to his jaws. All eyes were on the Malice. Only Mirabelle could see the birds on the wall take to the sky. A handful at first.

It felt right, that's what she thought to herself as the first raven slammed into the Malice. The raven landing on her shoulder had somehow felt *right*.

The raven hit the Malice in the side of the face, a glancing blow but enough to cause it to drop Gideon. Gideon scampered up the steps and straight into the arms of Eliza.

The Malice looked enraged. It took a step toward Mirabelle, a clawed hand outstretched. It opened its tooth-filled maw.

"You will—"

Another raven hit him. This one with the force of a bullet. The Malice put a clawed hand to its cheek, not quite believing what was happening. Another raven hit, then another. Each one collided with a loud, percussive smack.

Mirabelle looked at the wall. A cloud of ravens rose up. They flew over the estate. They circled and shrieked, cawing as they went round and round above the crowd. The Malice looked up and snarled.

Mirabelle looked at the one-eyed raven and nodded. He cawed. She looked at the cloud of ravens, and she willed them downward.

They descended in a black cloud of fury, hammering the Malice straight into the dirt. One wave followed after another, until the creature was pummeled into the ground. They ripped and they shredded, tearing away bits of flesh. Mirabelle saw a claw severed from its limb and felt a little dart of pleasure as the Malice screamed. She looked at her family and friends, all stunned by the scene before them. Dotty and Daisy were standing with mouths agape.

"Look, Daisy," Mirabelle shouted. "I *can* do something."

She raised her arms, then drove the birds downward. The ravens responded like musicians to a conductor. It looked as if they were attempting to hammer the Malice right through the earth. They became a black tornado of whirring feathers and snapping beaks, a maelstrom of fury and flashing eyes. Mirabelle watched them, willed them on. Down they came again and again, snapping and biting and pounding. Then finally Mirabelle closed her eyes and nodded, and they rose up as one, flew up into the night sky, and dispersed.

Mirabelle opened her eyes. The eerie silence was broken only by the fluttering of the raven on her shoulder, and the wet *gug-gug* hissing and gurgling sounds of the creature that lay before her.

She advanced toward it. All that remained of the Malice was a skeletal thing with bits of white flesh hanging from it. It looked like the carving on the door with even more flesh sloughed off its body, except it still had its vile head with its gray slimy eyes and yellow teeth.

Mirabelle stood over it. It raised its one remaining claw as if begging for mercy. Mirabelle went down on one knee and took its head delicately between her hands and looked into its eyes.

"I've been feeling this terrible pain ever since we first met."

The creature tried to turn its head away, but it was too weak. It made a moist choking sound, as if it were trying to speak.

"Shush now. I think I know what the pain was. I'd never felt it before, you see."

Mirabelle closed her eyes and opened her mouth and took in a great lungful of air through her nose. The Malice started to tremble, and a dark flickering mist started to rise from its body, collecting into a round revolving core above it. Mirabelle took that strange darkness in her hands. She brought it toward her mouth. The creature keened and wept, but Mirabelle paid it no heed.

She swallowed its black soul.

The remains of the Malice collapsed into a spiky wet mush of bones and melted gray flesh. Mirabelle wiped an arm across her mouth. The raven cawed. She stood up and turned to her family. She smiled at them.

"I was so hungry. But I'm not hungry anymore."

Part 5
Where and When

Jem

Jem and Tom were in the garden, helping Mirabelle plant flowers.

It was midmorning, and they'd sown at least a dozen. One or two had started sprouting, and one in particular had already reached a height of two feet and began snapping at them. It dived at Tom, and he barely twisted out of the way in time.

"Be careful," said Mirabelle. "You have to keep watching them. They're young and haven't learned any manners yet."

The seeds were huge, and to Jem they looked like veined and overgrown apple pips. They were so large that they had to be held with two hands. The air took on a metallic tang, and the hairs on Jem's forearms stood on end. Odd appeared beside her, clutching half a dozen more seeds to his chest. He was panting slightly. Jem was delighted to see him back on his feet. He'd made a quick recovery, and in the week since Mirabelle had defeated the Malice, Odd had come on in leaps and bounds and was back to his old wandering ways.

He handed Jem two seeds. "These ones are just about to pop, so I would suggest planting them quite soon."

By "quite soon" Jem knew Odd meant "right now."

Odd doled out the seeds, then stood with his hands behind his back, surveying everything, rocking back and forth on his heels.

"You could help, Odd," said Mirabelle on her knees, shoveling soil aside.

Odd gave the subtlest shake of his head, as if he'd barely heard her. "I source things, Mirabelle. That is my unenviable task."

Jem frowned at him. He looked pensive, as if his mind wasn't really present. It took him a while to notice her staring at him, and he just gave her a quick nod and went back to rocking on his heels, occasionally saying something like "That pod is going to be trouble—I can tell."

Jem reasoned that he was probably worrying about the meeting going on with the council right now. They were discussing what Enoch had called a "new Covenant." Jem had no idea what that entailed, but Mirabelle seemed optimistic about it and told her there was nothing to worry about thanks mainly to Piglet. Because of Piglet everyone understood each other now, she said. There were no barriers, no lies, no pretenses, no hatreds. Meanwhile, Piglet was safely back in his room, presumably content because his ration of meat had been almost doubled. It was being sourced mainly by Odd, who was now also providing some supplies to the village.

"Where do you get them?" asked Tom.

Odd's mind still seemed to be elsewhere, but he managed to answer. "I can't tell you that. If I told you that, your mind would be overthrown, you would go mad, the world would seem to you to be nothing but—"

"Odd," said Mirabelle sharply.

"What?"

"Stop talking."

Odd nodded, looking so serious that Jem almost laughed.

There was a caw from a tree branch overhead where the one-eyed raven looked down from his perch. He always seemed to be with Mirabelle now.

"You see," said Mirabelle. "Lucius agrees with me."

Everyone laughed, except Odd, who just frowned at the raven. Mirabelle had christened him Lucius after a Roman general. Odd didn't like it, but Jem thought it seemed to suit the raven with his haughty bearing.

The back door opened, and Freddie came out.

"They're finished," he said.

"What did they decide?" asked Mirabelle, straightening up and brushing soil off her dress.

"To continue as before," he said, "but that there should be greater trust and that your family are permitted to visit the village any time."

"Really?" said Odd.

"Yes," said Freddie.

Odd thought about this for a moment. "Why would anyone want to go to the village?"

Mirabelle punched him on the arm. "Odd!"

"Sorry," he said. "I didn't mean to be rude."

Enoch, Dr. Ellenby, and Mr. Teasdale approached from the house.

"How goes the planting?" asked Enoch.

"I've only been bitten once," said Tom, holding up a hand with a purple bruise on it.

"Well, so long as you don't get eaten," said Enoch.

"Was that a joke, Uncle?" asked Mirabelle.

Enoch didn't seem to know how to answer.

Odd shook his head in amazement. "Remarkable how things change. I think you're growing as a person, Uncle. I applaud the new you."

Dr. Ellenby chuckled to himself, and Enoch looked at him and narrowed his eyes.

Enoch cleared his throat. "Mr. Teasdale has something to say."

Mr. Teasdale stepped forward, fidgeting with his fingers. "Firstly, I would like to apologize to you, Mirabelle. I unjustly accused you of something that you did not do. Secondly . . ."

Jem was surprised to see his eyes welling up with tears.

"Secondly I would like to thank you personally, and on behalf of the people of Rookhaven for what you did." He turned to look at Jem. "I think we owe this young lady a great debt too. Miss Griffin, if it hadn't been for your quick thinking . . ." He wiped a hand across his eyes, but it was too late. "I'm sorry," he sobbed, "I'm a little overcome."

"That's all right, Mr. Teasdale," said Mirabelle.

"How's Mr. Tibbles, Mr. Teasdale?" asked Tom.

Mr. Teasdale looked surprised and then oddly grateful that Tom had asked after his cat. He smiled broadly now. "Very well, thank you for asking. He is, however, slightly on the mischievous side."

Tom nodded politely as Mr. Teasdale proceeded to go on at length about his cat. Dr. Ellenby looked at his watch. "My, my, is that the time? We should be getting back."

Mr. Teasdale started to follow him as they made their way toward the garden gate. Dr. Ellenby turned round and winked at everyone, then did a little clap.

"Well done again, Mirabelle, and Jem Griffin from London."

All eyes were on Enoch now. He stood with his hands behind his back and nodded.

"Well now."

"Well now indeed, Uncle," said Odd.

There was a slight pause.

Enoch cleared his throat. "It has been decided that Jem and Tom can stay in the house. Indefinitely."

Jem felt a warm glow as both Tom and Mirabelle grinned at her.

"You will, of course, pull your weight. There is dusting to do, polishing and whatnot."

"And whatnot. Whatnot is very important," said Odd.

"Yes, well . . ." Enoch looked at them all as if he couldn't quite figure out how to leave.

Mirabelle stepped forward and stood before him.

"Thank you, Uncle. Thank you for everything you've done for me."

Enoch looked a little taken aback, but then he held out his hands and clasped Mirabelle's in his.

"And thank *you*, Mirabelle," he said, smiling down at her.

He turned and went back into the house.

"I should go—my dad's waiting for me," said Freddie. He smiled and headed for the front of the house.

Lucius cawed. Mirabelle looked at the sky. "Looks like rain."

"Good, then we can go inside," said Odd. He started toward the house. He stopped when he realized no one was following. "Come on," he said. "You won't get a second invitation."

Jem thought he seemed troubled. He was frowning so hard he looked as if he were in pain.

"Where to?" she asked.

Odd squirmed a little, as if something prickly was stuck under his jacket. "My room," he said, avoiding their eyes.

"Your room?" gasped Mirabelle.

Odd looked slightly exasperated. "Yes."

"But no one—"

"'Goes with Odd.' Yes, I know, dear Mirabelle. And no

one has ever seen my room, but I'm asking you all to come with me now because I have something I want to show you."

Mirabelle and Jem exchanged a glance. They were both intrigued.

"All right, then," said Mirabelle brightly.

They all headed toward the house. Mirabelle raised her hand. "Come on, Lucius."

Lucius twitched his wings for a moment, but stayed on his tree branch.

"Lucius?"

Odd looked apologetic. "I think he knows."

Mirabelle frowned. "Knows what?"

"He knows he can't go where you're going. Not this time."

Freddie

They had left the house behind and Freddie's father was driving down the road that led into Rookhaven. He shifted slightly in his seat as he drove.

"I think it went well," he said.

Freddie was a bit taken aback. His father never initiated a conversation, and this was very definitely the start of one.

"What, Dad?"

"The discussions. I think they went well. You know you can go up to the house at any time now to visit your friends."

There was a pause as Freddie tried to comprehend what was being said.

"Any time," his father said, nodding resolutely to himself, his eyes on the road.

"Thanks, Dad."

There was another long but slightly more panicked pause. Freddie didn't know where to look.

"I was very proud of him, you know."

Freddie looked at his father.

"I was too, Dad."

His father looked at him, his eyes shining. "And he was proud of you." He looked back at the road. Freddie felt as if his chest and head were expanding. He felt as if he might burst.

"We should go fishing again," his father said.

The last time they'd been fishing was with James. Freddie hadn't thought about that day in years, and now it came flooding back. The warm, gentle breeze through the reeds, the sunlight on the water, James showing him how to cast his line.

"Mum should come too," he said.

"A good idea. We can make a picnic of it," his dad said.

Freddie watched the road ahead, and he smiled.

Mirabelle

Odd's room was chaotic and cavernous. Things were jumbled everywhere. There were paintings and clocks, various ornaments, several chandeliers, fur rugs, a penny-farthing, a collection of suitcases, a velvet smoking jacket, a rather lurid gold ballgown, a suit of armor, a couple of spiky maces, a wooden shield, dozens of snow globes. A giant stuffed tortoise hung from the ceiling, and Mirabelle found a full-sized stuffed mammoth particularly intriguing. A mounted moose's head attracted Tom.

"Look at me—I'm a moose," he said, holding it in front of his face.

"Yes, yes, very droll," said Odd, standing before a wooden table and looking around agitatedly.

Jem gave Mirabelle a questioning look. She knew something was up too.

"What is it, Odd? What's going on?" asked Mirabelle.

Odd nibbled the tip of his index finger, then wagged it in the air like a professor about to embark on a lecture.

"I wanted to show you something."

He rummaged in his jacket pocket and took out the gold chain that Mirabelle had seen before. He put it on the table, and Mirabelle stepped forward to look at it more closely.

It was a golden necklace with a charm in the shape of a loop. It was simple but very pretty.

"That's lovely," said Mirabelle.

"This necklace was your mother's," said Odd, looking very serious.

Mirabelle was surprised. "My mother's? Where did you get it?"

"She gave it to me for safekeeping."

Mirabelle picked up the necklace. Tom and Jem crowded around to have a look.

"It's beautiful," said Jem.

"It's expensive," said Tom.

Jem narrowed her eyes at him.

Mirabelle held it tight for a moment, remembering the woman she'd seen in her visions with Piglet.

"Where did she get it?" asked Mirabelle.

Odd cleared his throat. "That's the thing. It was a gift. And I think she got it from you."

Mirabelle was gobsmacked. "What?"

The three of them looked bemused as they stood in front of Odd.

"Let me attempt to explain," he said. He rummaged around in his pocket again and brought out the lump of soap and arrowhead he'd previously shown Mirabelle. He put them on the bench.

"This is soap. And this is an arrowhead."

They all stepped closer for a look.

"The thing is," said Odd, "this is ancient Babylonian soap, and this is a Saxon arrowhead."

Tom picked up the arrowhead. "But this looks brand-new, and the soap . . . the soap looks like it was made yesterday."

"Yes," said Odd.

Mirabelle's mind was spinning. "What are you getting at, Odd?"

"'No one goes with Odd,' that's what everyone says, but that has been disproven by recent dramatic events, and despite my private nature I've had to forgo tradition and allow people to travel with me."

Mirabelle could feel her impatience building. She had a sense of something at play, but—like an unfinished jigsaw—it just didn't make sense yet. She was waiting for the final piece to click into place.

"When I travel, it's not just a matter of where, although that geographic measurement is very often the only relevant factor, but sometimes it can be a matter of *when*."

They all stared at him. Nobody moved.

Odd lifted the arrowhead. "I'm three hundred years old, give or take a decade or two, but I picked this up at the Battle of Hastings in 1066." He held up the soap. "And I borrowed this from a nobleman in ancient Babylon."

Mirabelle held her breath. They were all frozen in place.

"Right," said Tom, shaking his head, "but you're *only* three hundred years old."

Mirabelle's eyes narrowed. "You said my mother got this necklace from me."

"That's what I've surmised," said Odd.

"But I've never met my mother."

Odd nodded. "Your mother appeared with the necklace one day. I think it was about a week or two into her stay with us. Enoch inquired politely as to where she'd got it, and she told him she'd met a young girl in the garden who'd given it to her. The young girl had black hair and wore dark velvet clothes."

Mirabelle felt momentarily light-headed and had to lean on the table.

"You have met your mother, Mirabelle, just not yet." Odd frowned. "Or at least you have, but you haven't . . . it's all very confusing."

Odd looked at them all, and to Mirabelle it seemed as if a great weight had been lifted off his shoulders. He took in a deep breath. "Now, who would like to go with Odd?"

It was different this time.

When Mirabelle stepped through the portal with Odd, Jem, and Tom, she felt less of a rushing sensation and more of a feeling of just passing over a threshold.

They found themselves in the secluded portion of the garden that curved round the back of the house. Odd pointed toward a bush and signaled for them to creep low toward it. It was a sunny day, and the air felt fresher. The house looked cleaner and less tangled with thorns and ivy. Mirabelle was still trying to take it all in when Odd tapped her on the shoulder and told them to watch.

A woman dressed in white was sitting on a bench, reading a book. Mirabelle recognized her instantly. Her heart started to pound, and she began to tremble.

"Odd, I can't do this. This is just . . ."

Odd put the necklace in her hand and gently closed her fingers round it.

"It's all right, Mirabelle. You've done it already." His brow furrowed. "Or at least you will. The truth is, I'm getting a slight headache thinking about it."

Mirabelle launched herself at him and squeezed him tight. "Thank you, Odd."

Odd patted her on the back, his voice muffled against her neck. "You're welcome."

Mirabelle hugged Tom next, which took him by surprise. She reserved her strongest hug for Jem.

"Thank you, Jem, for everything."

"I didn't do anything," said Jem, pulling away and wiping her eyes.

Mirabelle shook her head. "That's not true."

"Go to her," Jem said.

Mirabelle nodded and steeled herself. She clutched the necklace tightly in her fist, then walked out from behind the bush.

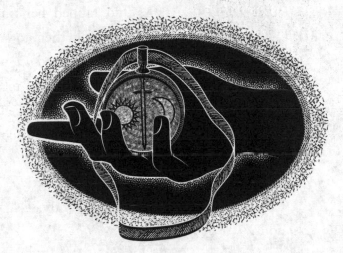

Her legs felt like lead, and her heart was pounding even harder.

She saw the woman turn. Saw her smile.

Mirabelle suddenly felt as if she were floating on air.

And now she stood before her mother. She had gray eyes and dark hair.

"Hello," her mother said.

"Hello," said Mirabelle.

"What's your name?" she asked.

"I'm Mirabelle."

"Mirabelle. That's a lovely name. My name's Alice."

"I know," said Mirabelle.

Piglet

Piglet sees everything now.

He sees the people of Rookhaven.

He sees Alfie Parkin approaching the baker's, clutching a bunch of flowers. He can hear Alfie's heart beating fast just before he opens the door. He can see the look of delight on Amy's face when the door opens.

He sees Mr. and Mrs. Smith working in the greengrocery. Mr. Smith stops what he's doing for a moment and stares at the photo of his sons on the wall. Mrs. Smith goes to him and squeezes his hand.

He sees Dr. Ellenby sauntering up the main street. People salute him as he passes by, and he greets them warmly in return. Then Dr. Ellenby stops with his hands in his pockets and looks around at the village, and Piglet can see the pride in his eyes.

He sees the Fletchers by the river. Mrs. Fletcher is sitting on a picnic blanket. She watches Mr. Fletcher and Freddie bait their fishing hooks. Mr. Fletcher ruffles Freddie's hair and Mrs. Fletcher smiles.

Piglet can see the house too. He can see Enoch looking out over the estate, a faint look of satisfaction on his face. He sees Eliza in front of her dressing table, examining her makeup in the mirror. Dotty and Daisy are dancing and singing in the Room of Knives, and Piglet can tell the ravens aren't impressed but they tolerate it.

And because Piglet doesn't belong to time and space, because Piglet is different, he also sees the house at a different time, at a time when he was younger.

He sees Odd, Jem, and Tom hiding behind a bush. He sees Mirabelle tentatively approaching a woman sitting on a bench. He can hear Mirabelle's heart pounding.

Now Piglet rolls over. He is very tired from all his recent exertions, and he just wants to rest for a bit. But before he goes to sleep Piglet smiles as he thinks of Mirabelle and the woman.

Because now Piglet knows what love is.

Acknowledgments

I want to thank everyone at Macmillan Children's Books for their help in getting my book into the world and into readers' hands. Special thanks to Venetia Gosling for her wonderful editing, her professionalism, and her attention to detail. My thanks to Lucy Pearse too, for her incredibly helpful insights and her hard work behind the scenes. I'd also like to thank Jo Hardacre and the whole communications team for all their help. Thanks also to Christian Trimmer at Henry Holt and Company for his input and feedback. I'm eternally grateful to all of you for your help during these very strange circumstances, especially at a time when things couldn't have been easy for anybody.

Special thanks to Edward Bettison for his breathtaking illustrations, which have turned my humble book into something that looks and feels truly special. Thanks also to Tracey Ridgewell for her beautifully designed interiors and to Art Director Rachel Vale for her cover design and help in getting the book to look as wonderful as it does. Thank you also to Lelia Mander and Sherri Schmidt for your help with the edits in this edition.

I'd like to acknowledge the assistance provided by the

Arts Council of Ireland in enabling me to finish this book. I'm very grateful for their help.

Thanks once again to my agent, the incomparable Sophie Hicks. Sophie, you are one in a million.

I'd like to thank my friends and family for all their support in the past few years. A special thank you to everyone who came to my book launches; it's something I always appreciate.

Inspiration sometimes comes from the most unexpected places. I came across the music of Hilary Woods at just the right time, and it helped me unlock the story of Mirabelle and Jem. Thank you for that, Hilary.

And lastly, a special thank you to Trevor Malone for helping out at the very beginning. Cheers, Trev.

About the Author

Pádraig Kenny is an Irish writer from County Kildare, now living in Limerick with his wife and four children. Previously an arts journalist, a teacher, and a librarian's assistant, he now writes full-time.

His first novel, *Tin*, was a Waterstones Book of the Month and was nominated for the Carnegie Medal, as well as being shortlisted for the Irish Book Awards and several regional awards. *The Monsters of Rookhaven* is his first novel with Macmillan Children's Books.

About the Illustrator

Edward Bettison is a graphic designer and illustrator, born in Hull, England. After studying graphic design at Nottingham Trent University, he moved to London to work in the music industry and then on to publishing.

He is known for the intricate detail in his original works, authenticity of vision, and bold imagery.

He lives in Brighton with his partner, Susannah, and his son, Kip.